Daniel Ricketson

The Autumn Sheaf

a collection of miscellaneous poems

Daniel Ricketson

The Autumn Sheaf
a collection of miscellaneous poems

ISBN/EAN: 9783337370909

Printed in Europe, USA, Canada, Australia, Japan

Cover: Foto ©Andreas Hilbeck / pixelio.de

More available books at **www.hansebooks.com**

THE

AUTUMN SHEAF:

A COLLECTION OF

MISCELLANEOUS POEMS.

BY

DANIEL RICKETSON.

NEW BEDFORD:
PUBLISHED BY THE AUTHOR.
1869.

E. ANTHONY & SONS, Printers, New Bedford.

DEDICATION.

WHOSO delights in quiet paths to stray,
　　To whom the Muses lend their kindly aid;
Who shuns the glare of Ostentation's sway,
　　Within whose court a worship base is paid;
　　Whose soul by Nature's gentler voice is stayed:
To these my Muse would dedicate her strains,
　　Unmarked by classic lore or guileful art,
The simple music of the hills and plains, —
　　And thus give pleasure to some kindred heart,
　　That seeks to draw from life its better part.

THE AUTUMN SHEAF.

NOW in the waning years of life,
   Since Autumn crowns my lengthened days,
Apart from scenes of worldly strife,
   And seeking light from Wisdom's ways,
I've gathered up from far and near
   The records of my joy and grief,
And with a mingled hope and fear,
   Have bound them in an AUTUMN SHEAF.

D. R.

Brooklawn, near New Bedford,
   April 1, 1869.

CONTENTS.

SECOND SERIES. 1856–1869.

CONTENTS.

ERRATA.

Page 284, line 15, for arm, read smith.
Page 284, line 21, for Stands one, read He stands.

FIRST SERIES.

1836—1856.

PROEM.

COULD I portray in fair and easy verse
        The features of my own New England home,
The phases of her seasons, what I 've seen
And felt within her pleasant haunts
Of wood and field, by stream or lake,
In lonely places, and the valued truths
I oft have found arise therefrom, then I
Might hope to leave a record that would cheer
Others more youthful in life's pilgrimage.
Such seems, howe'er, to be the lot of man,
That revelations made to one rarely
Can be conveyed to others; each himself
Must find the treasure Nature offers all;
Still I shall venture to attempt the task,
And from the storehouse of my musing hours,
Though all unequal to my heart's desire
Bring forth its humble wares as best I may,
In the fond hope thereby to contribute
A modest portion to the common weal,
And thus not useless prove my walk in life.

    1860.

HOPES OF YOUTH.

O SHOULD my life be spared to age,
   Though age bring with it pain,
May scenes that now my youth engage,
   Still with me then remain.

May still the landscape smile for me,
   That smiles on all around ;
And seated 'neath some favorite tree,
   As now, be often found, —

Whose spreading branches overhead,
   A canopy shall lend ;
And may I feel, though youth hath sped,
   Joy with my sorrow blend.

And though my limbs should need the aid
   Of kindly arm, or staff,
Still may I seek the woodland shade,
   The crystal streamlet quaff, —

There in the glass of memory dwell
 Upon the varied past;
And if a sigh my heart should swell,
 Still may the vision last.

May still the sight of cheerful youth
 My heart's blood stir with glee,
And still the force of simple truth
 Its blessings bring to me.

May sweet religion lend her aid
 To cheer life's waning hour,
And on the " Rock of ages " stayed,
 May I then feel its power, —

Its power to smooth the brow of care,
 And cheer the pilgrim's way,
To light up all the cells of thought,
 As in youth's blithesome day.

1839.

SIMPLE PLEASURES.

NOT in the decorated halls of wealth,
　　Where flows the goblet round the groaning board,
While the old walls re-echo to the mirth
That maddened senses rudely vaunt aloud,
Is pleasure, such as cheers the heart's blood, found ;
But in the calmer scenes of Nature's court,
In woodland shades, beside the murmuring rill
Or tumbling waterfall, or meadows gay,
Where, undisturbed by aught that man defiles,
The works of God speak forth his majesty.
Here the rapt soul can soar to other realms,
And bathe in light from His eternal throne,
Who in His works demands our reverent love.

THE SPIRIT OF POETRY.

O THOU blest influence, mighty, undefined!
  Yet everywhere abroad through the wide earth,
And filling all with thy unceasing charm:
Thou not alone dost dwell in sombre wood,
Or by the flowery bank of crystal stream,
Or waterfall, or roaring cataract;
But thou dost grace the lowly cottage roof,
And throwest a charm around the cheerful board;
Thou hoverest o'er the village church-yard's calm,
And seemest to mourn o'er virtue early lost,
And e'er to innocence thou lendest thy smile;
Thou fillest with hope the wanderer's lonely way,
When thoughts of home come o'er his sorrowing soul,
And his roused pulses leap to take him there.
There is no voice in Nature's wide domain,
But thou, sweet Spirit, dost it aye pervade,
E'en to the lowliest insect's gentle hum;
And thou art mighty, when around the throne
Of God's omnipotence sublime, employed!
With what a beauty to the soul then comes
The word of peace, with inspiration filled!

Then the sweet Psalmist's, and the Prophet's voice
Have a far greater and more winning force.
True piety is ever filled with thee,
And all that once in chilling garb appeared,
Now warms the soul with aspirations deep.
Without thee, this fair world were but a blank,
A cold, unwished-for resting place : —
Yes ! thou dost come from His all-forming hand
Who framed the vast universe ; and who gave
Thy potent sway to beautify his works.
And then, O thoughtful man ! wilt thou be dull
To the rich influence of fair Nature's claim,
Or to her voice that now within thee calls,
Prompting thy soul to soar above this earth,
And fix her pinions in the realms of grace?
O, rather listen to " the still, small voice,"
And listening obey, for it is Truth to thee.

1837.

EVENING REVERY.

BE with me, Muse! my ever constant friend,
  Whose influence sweet can soothe my loneliest
      hour,
And as to thee with reverence I bend,
  Still on my head thy genial spirit pour.

And now, as silently the guards of night,
  The fresh-lipped moon, and all her bright array,
In softened smiles send forth their mellow light,
  O, trace with me, my Muse, our cherished way.

For thou in childhood on my infant breast,
  Ere Reason had assumed her tyrant sway,
Thy potent charms hadst lastingly impressed,
  And lit my path with thy enkindling ray.

Then, led by thee, fair Nature's haunts I sought,
  At early morn, at noon, and dewy eve,
And felt what ne'er philosophy had taught —
  The glowing raptures thou for me didst weave.

How fresh, and fair, each rural thicket gleamed!
　Where mingled notes at early morning broke,
Ere yet day's orb aslant the hill-top beamed,
　Or weary rustics from their dreams awoke.

And thou bright moon, that watched o'er all below,
　How grateful would my heart to thee ascend!
When pensively reclined beneath yon brow,
　Where oft to meet thee I my steps would bend.

There I would love to trace the mystic band,
　That walk Heaven's arch when thou remountest thy
　　　car,
In grand obeisance to the all-guiding Hand,
　Seen here, around, and in yon vault afar.

And shall time snatch aught of my youthful taste?
　Shall the rude world this heart congeal, or chill?
Rather this form should crumble into waste,
　Than simple Truth its spirit cease to fill.

And thou my Muse, still lend thy welcome aid,
　To smooth the cares of life that time must bring;
And when upon death's lowly bed I'm laid,
　Be with thee as in life's earliest spring.

1838.

THE GOOD TIME.

WHEN nations wise shall learn to war no more,
  And man o'er man release his tyrant power,
And the fair earth in radiant beauty shine,
As was intended by the Hand divine;
When man in native strength shall go forth free,
And the loud chorus sound from sea to sea,
The glorious anthem of his liberty;
Then shall the mountains skip like agile rams,
And every hill rejoice like playful lambs;
At morning's dawn the music shall awake,
Nor shall the evening shades its freshness break.
O, happy day, and happy they who dwell
Upon the earth when such glad tidings swell!
As sang the Prophet in the days of old,
Whose words still ring throughout the world like gold,
The sword to ploughshares then shall moulded be,
And every one sit 'neath his vine and tree.
No cruel master shall the weak upbraid,
None shall molest him, none shall make afraid,
For thus the Lord hath in his wisdom spoken,
And on mankind bequeathed the sacred token.

THE OLD LIBRARY.

AMID your classic shades, old favorite haunt,
  Again as erst with reverent steps I roam,
While o'er my mind, like some sweet spirit chant,
  From heavenly spheres your kindly voices come.

Here in my boyhood's meditative hours,
  With truant steps alone I ofttimes strayed ;
And loved to court the ever-witching powers
  That round your hallowed seat supremely played.

Old friends, I hail ye ! so unlike the chill
  Of the world's selfishness and unconcern,
Your potent charms the soul with rapture fill,
  And move its depths with love of truth to burn.

How oft beneath your genial grace I pored
  With welcome toil o'er some inspired page !
While my young heart with strange emotions soared,
  And swelled its bounds with philosophic rage.

Not all a dream was that, my boyish gaze,
  For though no tutored hand my course did guide,

B2

Much I obtained amid the lettered maze,
  That still I keep with reverential pride.

Here first I learned with cherished love to burn
  O'er mighty Milton's soul-exalting page;
And now with fervor which doth oft return,
  I love to dwell on the great poet-sage.

And thou dear bard, old England's honest pride,
  With what delight thy beauties to me came!
Thou who my early footsteps oft did'st guide:
  My heart still leaps at Cowper's hallowed name.

Here too I loved with pensive Gray to muse,
  While to his solemn strains my pulses beat;
Or Goldsmith's sweet inspiring page peruse,
  And with him 'mid the towering Alps retreat.

And other bards that to my soul are dear,
  Here first I learned their magic sway to prize,
Around whose names the glories sparkle clear,
  Whose praise has risen to the far-stretched skies.

And I would not forget those youthful days,
  For they like sunshine o'er my spirit spread,
And lead me still through many pleasant ways,
  Though boyhood's hours for me long since have fled.
1836.

THE FALLEN WOOD.

YE brave old woods, farewell! who have so long,
    Spread your huge branches to the wintry wind,
Or waved your leafy tops 'neath summer's breeze;
Within whose still retreats, the gentle band
Of Nature's choristers has nestled oft,
And hatched their young, and sung their mellow chants.
Farewell! the woodman's axe hath laid ye low,
And soon upon some sturdy yeoman's hearth,
Or that of well-fed citizen, ye'll blaze.
No more by eager fancy borne along,
Far from the cares that crowd the haunts of man,
Shall I commune within your quiet walks,
Which seemed so hidden from the glare of day,
That ages might have passed you undisturbed.
But the all-grasping hand of gain hath found you,
And ye have fallen. That aged raven,
Sweeping his lonely way o'er your sad ruins,
In vain seeks out his once sequestered nest,
And boding omens sad, sends forth his tale
Of sorrow. Where is the heart that cannot feel
A pain to see fair Nature thus disrobed?

So it was not meant — God lends the leafy grove,
And the grand influence of the forest wild,
To calm our worldly nature, and to tranquilize
The troubled waters of the harassed soul.
But man, not heeding Nature's kindly boon,
Blots her fair face, and treats her oft with scorn.
The pleasant Spring has come, and o'er your haunts
Casts its broad smile.   An effort yet for life
You make, and from your sad and mutilated stumps,
Shoots forth the juicy twig.   But years must pass,
The yet unwrinkled brow must droop with age,
Those limbs, now strong and in the flush of youth,
Must shrink and weaken neath the hand of time,
Or moulder in the cold damp vault of earth,
Ere ye shall rear your lordly heads again.
Methinks yon warbler by his saddened note
Laments your fate, and in his soft complaint
Would call unfeeling man to his hard lot.
Man is a destroyer! before whose might
The lofty forests fall — earth, sky, and water,
All must yield to him — for so the word is written.
" Deep calleth unto deep," and oft within
The far recesses of the solemn wood,
A voice like that which at Creation's birth
Spread o'er the forming world, may then be heard ;

And to the soul so clear, so deep, it comes,
That man might deem the great Jehovah spake,
Prompting his wayward thoughts to look above,
And lost in wonder, worship and adore.
Then let the groves remain ! sacred to thought,
To purity, to health, and sweet devotion ;
Where rural worshipper may steal away,
Far from the jarring world where Mammon reigns,
That world which oft has caused his heart to mourn,
And droop with sadness ; here let him come,
And pour out the full tide of his feelings
In free communion with the God of all.
Here in her beauty let the maiden come,
Blushing to hear the low repeated vows
Of him for whom she lives.   What fitter place
For pure, congenial hearts to sympathize?
The man of sorrow too may linger here,
And in the solemn stillness of these scenes,
Find a sure balm to heal his wounded heart,
And bid him think that life may yet be blessed.
Spare then the grand old woods, the pleasant groves,
And delve the earth, — there borrow from the mine
The sulphurous lump to cheer the winter hearth.

1839.

KITCHEN MUSINGS.

I LOVE by the warm kitchen wood-fire to ponder,
   While thick-coming fancies envelop my mind,
And the old chimney rumbles like far distant thunder,
   A trumpet alarm of the god of the wind.

The casements all rattle, and threaten to tumble;
   They've told the same tale these odd fifty years:
I heed it no more than old Boreas' grumble;
   To the chicken-heart only it brings any fears.

Let all those who wish, sit ensconced in the parlor;
   In vain they attempt their gloom to deceive:
I rather would hum some old song of Kit Marlow
   By the warm kitchen wood-fire on a cold winter's eve.

O, the old kitchen hearth, the charm of my childhood!
   With fondness I hold to its generous heat:
It tells me of tales in the night-shrouded wildwood,
   And youthful emotions my fancy still greet, —

When entranced I sat by the warm glowing embers,
   And listened with tears to some heart-touching tale,

Which with fond cherished love my heart still remem-
    bers,
  For innocence then did o'er it prevail.

The simplest of pleasures are surely the sweetest, .
  And those which will bring the best good to the mind,
And though we deplore they so often prove fleetest,
  We still look with fond hope to those left behind.

1838.

SONNET — CHARLES LAMB.

HOW gloriously around thy cherished name,
    The gentle graces of thy soul are wreathed!
Each passing thought, or word but by thee breathed,
Is now recorded with thy lustrous fame.
O! happy they who had thee for a friend,
With whom thou fondly didst thy humor share,
And who as with one voice thy worth declare,
And aye with sorrow o'er thy ashes bend;
For thou possessed'st a spirit, rich and rare,
Which lasted to the evening of thy days,
As sunlight round some sparkling fountain plays;
And what of all most genial can combine,
This, gentle "Elia," was truly thine.

1838.

MY OLD PLAID CLOAK.

MY old plaid cloak! my old plaid cloak!
   How many storms we've borne together!
And now though old, and faded too,
   Thou still canst shield me from the weather.

And here thou art, old Tartan friend!
   Again brought out to face the blast,
And ward me from rude Boreas' cold,
   Faithful in duty to the last.

Yes! I have wrapped thee round my breast,
   And borne the brunt of many a storm;
And well hast thou withstood the test,
   But now art worn, and quaint in form;

Yet I'll not cast thee off, old friend,
   Dimmed as thou art, and beauty gone;
But every rent in thee will mend,
   Though thou shouldst cause the proud to scorn.

With thee my woodland walks I trace,
   When mantling snow is falling fast,

And safe within thy warm embrace,
    Fear naught from stern old Winter's blast.

Old Scottish plaid! thou bring'st to mind
    The thought of days long past and gone,
Of happy hours, and friendship kind,
    In memory blest, though erewhile flown.

Yet thou art here, my well-tried friend,
    Who half a score of years hast seen,
And wilt thy share of comfort lend,
    Though thou art not what thou hast been, —

A bonnie plaid, of fairest hue,
    That well might win the fair one's smile,
Of Lincoln green, and Highland blue,
    With purest white inmixed the while.

As on thy time-worn form I muse,
    My mind is turned to Scotia's land,
When Wallace brave, and gallant Bruce,
    In times of fear maintained command;

And fireside joys are brought to mind,
    With Bonnie Doon, and Auld Lang Syne,

And Highland lads, in bran-new plaids,
  Appear around thy hoary shrine.

Let who will call it weak in me,
  And smile at this my humble song,
Which thus records the worth of thee,
  Who hast been true to me so long, —

I cannot scorn thee, honest plaid!
  If thou art old, and faded too ;
For well thou hast my friendship paid,
  Nor shall my muse refuse thy due.

1836.

MY OLD PLAID CLOAK.

PART II.

AGAIN old Winter blusters round,
    With angry threats, and gusts full sour;
While chained with frost fast lies the ground,
    And overhead rude tempests lower.

Now from thy hiding place, old plaid!
    Again come forth as thou are wont;
The sight of thee still makes me glad;
    With thee I'll dare stern Winter's front.

In song I've called thee my old friend;
    Such thou hast ever proved to be;
And as through life my steps I wend,
    I'll strive to learn some truth of thee.

Since last I sang thy honest worth,
    Two years have rolled o'er sea and main,
Thousands of forms have sprung in birth,
    To taste this life of joy and pain.

How many in that rapid space,
　　Have o'er time's sweeping current sighed;
How many run their final race,
　　Bowed to the earth, and groaning, died.

But thou, old friend! remainest still
　　Amid earth's hurrying change and waste,
And I by His all bounteous will
　　Who rules the world, yet onward haste.

Still I can on thy merits muse,
　　And fill my mind with fancies sweet,
Still wrapped in thee some bard peruse,
　　And churlish Winter's raging greet.

But yet at times I mourn thy lot,
　　That thou to this drear Yankee land,
Away from thy dear native spot,
　　Hast come, as by some magic wand.

Better 't would seem that thou hadst clad
　　Some hardy son of Scotia's hills,
Who'd boasted thee his bonnie plaid,
　　And scorned the force of Highland chills, —

With him have clomb the rugged height
　　Of far-famed Grampian's snow-clad peak,

Or wandered by the pale moon's light,
　Loch Katrine's fairy-elf to seek.

But whist! thy fate I 'll not deplore,
　Far happier hast thou been with me:
With thee I yet may tread that shore,
　And all its wealth of beauty see.

Now rest awhile, my own goose-quill,
　And thou, old plaid, still lend thy cheer,
Still keep obedient to my will,
　Till Spring-time glads the circling year.

1838.

A WINTER SKETCH.

WHEN Winter's horn blows loud and clear,
   And snow drifts down the silent glen,
When slowly goes the waning year,
   And few of Nature's smiles are seen,
Then to the woods I often go,
Heedless alike of wind or snow.

'T is not when naught but smiles are seen,
   And fields are gay with new-blown flowers,
When the old woods are robed in green,
   That Nature shows her greatest powers ;
But when her hidden forces rise,
And clouds and storms deform the skies.

For then more boldly rush the streams,
   The waterfall more loudly roars,
And to the gale the raven screams,
   As o'er the lofty pines he soars.
And the riven branches loudly crack,
While echo sends the tumult back.

'T is then the mighty sea is tossed,
   And the frail bark to the tempest stoops,

When billows lash the rock-girt coast,
  Where the gray sea-gull slowly swoops;
And on the wind is often heard
The voice of some storm-driven bird.

Then far within the woods' retreat,
  With eager steps I gladly hie,
Where each familiar haunt I greet,
  As old friends in adversity.
For here a countless store I find,
That on me shed their influence kind.

The robin flits across my way,
  As though he would my coming hail,
The black-cap hops from spray to spray,
  And near by whirrs the startled quail;
While frisking on some neighboring bough,
The squirrel eyes me as I go.

The green moss peeps forth from the snow,
  And sweetly smiles at Winter's frown,
While with their load the maples bow,
  And humbly wear their winter crown.
Such rich reward kind Nature gives,
To him who in her quiet lives.

1838.

MY MOTHER'S GRAVE.

LONG hath thy pure spirit dwelt in sweet repose,
   My childhood's earliest, most endeared friend;
Yet my deep love for thee unceasing flows,
   And ever will till time with me shall end.

Strong are the ties that bind me unto thee,
   For they were formed at true affection's shrine,
When my young heart was as the wild breeze free,
   And fondly leaned its trusting hopes on thine.

I lost thee young, in boyhood's heedless hour,
   And mourned thee as a sorrow-stricken child,
Who hardly knew that death could wield his power
   O'er one so lovely, cherished, and mild:

But it was well, for thou hadst suffered pain,
   Such as might sunder all the ties of earth,
Though never were thy lips moved to complain,
   Or e'er to one desponding sigh gave birth.

And when upon thy dying bed thou lay'st,
   Thy last kind look, I yet distinctly see;

c

Though few and short the lingering words thou said' st,
 They will remain as seals of love from thee.

Though but a child, my loss I deeply felt,
 For to thy bosom all my troubles came;
And oft as by thy gentle side I knelt,
 I ever found thy ardent love the same.

Yet I but little knew how great the change
 That soon must o'er my future welfare come;
That I away should then be led to range,
 Afar from all the tender ties of home.

How often, then, while musing on my fate,
 In some sequestered haunt, or woodland shade,
Communing with the past, alone I've sat,
 And thought of thee beneath the cold turf laid.

And now, though manhood with its cares has come,
 Those youthful days I gladly cherish still;
And happy hours within my childhood's home,
 My yearning heart with strong emotions fill.

Thy gentle voice as wont I seem to hear,
 Thy welcome smile again I seem to see,

And household scenes again to me appear,
  Endeared as fond remembrances of thee.

But far from trouble thou art now away,
  Within those realms where only peace is found,
Where thou behold' st the light of that blessed day,
  From God's bright throne in splendor cast around.

1837.

THE BLIND MINSTREL.

FIRED at the thought, the minstrel struck his lyre,
  The chords resounded to his trembling hand,
And all around breathed out the holy fire,
  As when creation woke to God's command.

Up to the cross he turned his sightless eyes;
  He sung of Christ, his suffering, and death,
In tones ascending to the far-stretched skies,
  And borne to God by angels' holy breath.

His anxious soul had caught the living flame,
  And fondly strove to reach its destined height,
Where it might dwell with Him from whom it came,
  Who sits enthroned in pure ethereal light.

"Vain world!" he cried, "deceitful thou hast proved:
  When I was young, and fortune deigned to smile,
Then by my side were those I dearly loved;
  Now none are found, my sorrows to beguile.

"But there is hope — my Saviour is my friend;
  To him I turn, when sorrows crowd my soul:

He every harm will from my path defend,
  And gladly make my broken spirit whole."

And as beneath the aged elm he leant,
  Of childhood's sports so oft the happy scene,
Its waving boughs o'er him in beauty bent,
  And kindly shook its coronal of green.

Years had elapsed since last he left the spot;
  Long had he been a wanderer o'er the earth:
And now with pious heart he sought the spot
  Where the blest light of day shone on his birth.

His youthful friends within the ground were laid,
  And now a stranger in his boyhood's home,
Round its sweet haunts in solitude he strayed,
  While mingled thoughts o'er his worn spirit come.

But soon in yonder churchyard he shall lie,
  And o'er his head will thrive the senseless sod;
Yet though the tear oft fills his blighted eye,
  He has one friend to stay — that friend, his God.

1839.

MAY.

WHERE is the lovely month, the poets sing,
 With sweets profuse, and crowned with
  blushing flowers,
Which rural Thomson ycleped " gentle Spring ";
 The time when lovers sighed within green bowers,
 And poured their plaints as fell the pattering showers?
Long have they vanished, those delightful days ;
 Gone, gone for aye, those fond remembered hours.
No more for them the poet tunes his lays,
Nor to their once loved court his rare devotion pays.

Now wrapped in furs the stripling hastes along,
 At least in this our northern Yankee land ;
No Strephon here with Cloe joins his song,
 While Winter lingers with his chilling hand :
 But when fair Summer wields her magic wand,
Then lads and lassies you may many see,
 Wending their way beneath the moonlight flood,
While kindling love lights up the youthful eye,
And all around bespeaks the genial flow of joy.

No groups of happy children now are seen,
    Tracing the fragrant woodland paths along;
Nor by the brook that wells through meadows green,
    Is heard the laughter of the happy throng,
    Gathering fair flowers the scattered leaves among;
The swelling buds not yet their forms disclose,
    Nor yet is heard the Oriole's welcome song;
All nature shrinks beneath the Borean cold,
While yet storm-bearing Hyems doth his sceptre hold.

Yet soon the cheerful sun will venture forth,
    And smile on all the varied landscape round;
Then nature's charms will quickly spring in birth,
    And flowers adorn the now unmantled ground,
    And milder skies will for a time abound.
But though storm-wrapt our northern barriers stand,
    Kind heaven's best blessing may still here be found;
And gladly do I boast my native land,
And patiently will wait for airs and skies more bland.

1837.

THE PRIEST OF NATURE.

HARD by an old wood's still retreat,
    Whose bending boughs together meet,
An Indian sage alone doth dwell,
Within a rude embowered cell;
For he would choose to live alone,
Since all his early friends are gone.

Here oft I come upon my walk,
To hear the priest of nature talk;
For though he knew no classic shades,
Philosophy his soul pervades;
And every rock and tree around,
To him with mighty truths abound.

Once in this land his race was strong;
His fathers here did flourish long:
But now with population's tide,
They long since vanished from his side,
And he of all is left alone,
His once brave people to bemoan.

" Here," tearfully he oft will say,
" My earliest footsteps learned to stray ;
And often by this streamlet clear
My father's bow hath shot the deer,
While heedless from the verdant brink
He stooped his antlered head to drink.

" By yon old upland's shaggy side
Our wigwam rose in humble pride,
And here grew up my sisters fair,
Tall, comely maids, with long black hair ;
But they afar were early led,
And now are numbered with the dead.

" Yet still I love to linger here
Throughout the seasons of the year,
And every haunt I love to praise,
That met my childhood's eager gaze ;
Though often sad I musing stand,
And mourn o'er this my fathers' land.

" Woe be to that inglorious day
That swept our natal rights away,
And took from me my cherished bride,
Her aged father's hope and pride,

C2

And rudely snatched my sons from me,
To find their graves within the sea!

" And I will in this quiet stay ;
Here I my aged bones will lay :
Perhaps some friendly hand may place
A humble stone my grave to trace,
At which the traveller, passing by,
For my lone fate may drop a sigh,

" And haply to himself may say,
' Here a poor Indian lived his day,'
And sit him down beside the spot,
To think upon the red man's lot ;
O ! may his soul then rise in prayer,
That God our remnant small will spare."

Such was the old man's humble tale,
Told me within the secret vale ;
But higher themes he oft will raise,
And all his soul break forth in praise,
For fully to his simple heart
Kind Nature doth her power impart.

He will discourse of rocks, and trees,
Of birds, and flowers, the genial breeze,

And from their useful lessons prove
The present grace of boundless love;
For he mid Nature's wilds did learn,
Not e'en the smallest truth to spurn.

For him her mysteries have a voice,
Which makes his old heart oft rejoice,
And lessons from the well of Truth,
He learned to prize in early youth;
While now, with naught but Nature's fare,
He spends his lonely life in prayer.

1838.

DIGHTON ROCK.

WHENCE came these rude inscriptions? by whose
        hand
Was this old legend carved upon this rock,
Which hath so long withstood the shock of time?
Did some bold son of northern Europe here
Attempt to trace upon its time-worn face
A lasting record of his dauntless voyage?
Was it his mailed hand that cut these mystic forms,
Long ere Columbus landed on our shore,
Or bold Vespucius ploughed the briny deep?
Did some descendant of ·old Israel's tribe,
Who, wandering far, had crossed dark Behring's strait,
Rear his rude cabin here, and mark the spot,
That ages hence might read his chronicle,
And know his·sufferings? visionary thought!
Or as some deem, perhaps with reason, too,
That the swart Indian dwelling near these shores
In his rude sculpture wrought his simple tale,
And in uncouth numbers sang the pleasing song
Of the bold hunt, or when with light canoe
He skimmed this beauteous river, on whose sides

The lofty forest cast its cooling shades ;
Or of some murder 'neath the white man's roof,
From whence the reeking scalp in pride he brought, —
Sights that sent gladness to his savage heart.
Conjecture has been rife, and seems exhausted ;
But now a pilgrim to this ancient haunt,
I 'll sit me down amid these pleasant fields,
Beneath the branches of this spreading tree,
And muse upon the scene.   The ascending sun
Just peeps o'er yonder hill, before whose beams
The light mists fly ; and river's bank,
The dripping wood, and pebbly shore,
Glitter beneath his cheerful morning glance.
Anon the mist o'erpowers him, and again
He drives them off; and gathering strength
At each repeated effort, now at last
Throws his broad béams on all the landscape round.
The cottages, embosomed in green vales,
Peep forth as if to taste the sweets of day ;
Small hamlets, seated on the distant shore,
Appear in rural beauty, whose tall spires
Denote that God is there remembered.
The brown-thrush, perched on yonder topmost bough,
Chants clearly forth his joyous morning hymn,
And gentle murmurs from the insect race

Speak happiness where innocence abides.
And must I leave these scenes? must I again
Go forth amid the busy walks of men,
Where the proud worldling vaunts upon his stores,
And mimic statesmen talk their hearers deaf?
Yes, I must go.   Farewell! old legend rock,
Sweet river's bank; and thou, old boatman,
Who didst lend thy strength to land me here,
Farewell! thy honest heart would wither soon,
Amid the sordid ranks of human strife;
Still keep upon thy small, though hard-earned farm,
Nor learn the wiles that fill the noisy mart.
Come, now, good staff, companion of my way,
Lend thy kind aid, and I will journey on.

May, 1839.

THE OLD MEETING-HOUSE.

AY! there it stands, a melancholy pile,
   A rude memorial of olden days,
Yet here the cheering sunbeams sweetly smile,
   And the old roof receives their parting rays.
'T is sad to think of those who gathered there,
And humbly knelt before their God in prayer:

For scarcely one of that old race remains
   To tell the tale so sad, and yet so dear,
When health and pleasure filled their youthful veins,
   As fell the good man's words upon their ear;
And he hath gone unto the blessed land,
To join in praises with the holy band.

But memory fondly brings his worth to mind,
   And loves to linger round the honored sage,
For he was crowned with gifts we rarely find,
   And well could teach the great inspired page.
A faithful marble tells his place of rest,
And the tall grass waves o'er his reverent breast.

And that old graveyard, with its tumbling stones,
   That stays the traveller on his weary way,.

Who reads the lines above the mouldering bones,
   And feels 't is good in these lone haunts to stay, —
If any place could rouse the soul in prayer,
It must be here, where worship fills the air.

And there is one, a neat and lonely grave,
   That seems to throw a holy calm around :
The tale is short, and would no notice crave ;
   " Almira," only, marks the lowly mound :
Who could not drop a tributary tear,
Where fond affection's ties are seen so clear ?

If thou from earthly ills thy thoughts wouldst wean,
   And teach thy soul to muse on holy things,
Come here when twilight steals upon the scene,
   And feel thy spirit borne on seraph wings ;
For such repose pervades the spot around,
That thou wouldst seem to tread on holy ground.

No jar is here, with which the earth is rife,
   No pomp of pride to wound thy troubled breast,
Nor vain ambition, jealousy, or strife,
   Shall reach thee in this place of peaceful rest.
Here let me often, from the world away,
Steal a calm hour to muse at setting day.

1837.

CHARITY.

HAST thou a heart to feel another's woe, —
    To lend thy hand in misery's mournful cause?
Does its warm blood with deep emotions flow,
  When pity calls, nor heed the world's applause,
  Nor at its scoffs, or smiles, from virtue pause?
If so, thou much of bitter sights must bear,
  When suffering nature on thy kindness draws.
But press thou on! thy path is straight and clear;
A bounteous grace from high thy course will ever cheer.

Thou wilt not shun the poor man's lone abode,
  Where want and sickness fill his days with grief;
But guided by the wisdom of thy God,
  Thou gladly to his wants wilt bring relief.
  O Charity! of human good the chief,
From which the soul's best yearnings doth arise,
  Thou to the woes of life art never deaf,
But pure and reaching as the ambient skies!
O! well may mortal man thy high endowments prize.

1836.

THE VOICE OF NATURE.

SWEET voice of Nature ! thou dost come
   With healing balm unto the heart ;
Thou mak'st us feel this earth our home,
   And linger long ere we would part ; —
For in thy still retreats we see
Naught but the reign of harmony.

Whene'er we listen to thy voice,
   Or muse upon thy varied charms,
'T is then in life we should rejoice,
   And dwell within thy open arms, —
When with the haunts of man we tire,
And feel the good thou canst inspire.

That water-fall which wildly leaps
   With dashing course o'er yonder ridge ;
Those ponderous rocks in mighty heaps,
   That form a rude and fearful bridge, —
All, all in harmony combine,
And tell sweet Nature, they are thine.

Yon distant bell, that sweetly peals,
   Though swept by Winter rough and wild,

Like music on my ear now steals,
   And mellowed seems like nature's child ; —
Such is the power that dwells around,
Where'er thy magic voice is found.

And, too, the frost-bound, leafless trees,
   Like giants stripped of their attire,
Which answer to the sweeping breeze,
   Like ocean's voice or rush of fire, —
All speak a language to the heart,
That thou, O God ! dost these impart.

O Nature ! with what fond delight
   Thou to thy votaries dost seem ;
Though clothed in sombre robes of night,
   Nor lighted by the moon's fair beam,
Still thou hast beauties yet in store,
For him who would thy scenes explore.

Then what is luxury, or wealth,
   Compared with this that thou canst give?
A grateful heart — a glow to health —
   A moral lesson how to live, —
These, these are truths that will inspire
The heart that can thy works admire.

1837.

THE PILGRIM VOYAGE.

HIGH rolled the Atlantic waves; the fragile bark
    That bore the adventurous band of steadfast
      souls,
Mid ocean tossed, dashed onward to the coast,
That lay as yet beyond them many a league.
On, on they sail, day after day succeeds,
And naught but faith such as was felt of old
Upbears their weary limbs, to toils unused.
Ah! who can tell what grand results shall come
From that small group assembled on the deck,
Straining their eyes to catch the wished-for land?
There stands the manly form, the reverend sage,
The graceful matron, and the beauteous maid,
Born in some rural spot on England's shores,
Who oft have sported on the village green,
And slept beneath the peaceful cottage roof—
Home of their fathers, to remembrance dear.
The Sabbath passes, and no welcome sound
Of church-bell calls them to the house of God.
Around old ocean roars, and surging high
Threatens to engulf their strained and groaning bark.

Loud through the rigging howls the driving wind,
The bulwarks tremble, and the yards creak forth;
But from that cabin, where assembled now
These followers of Christ, ascends a voice,
That reaches far beyond the empyrean,
Even to the throne of Him who guides their way.
Their prayer is heard.   At last the long-sought shore
Heaves up to view, clothed in its wintry robe;
But land more welcome never met the eye
Of voyager wearied of old ocean's roar,
For there they see a shelter from the storm
That from the shores of Europe drove them hence —
A safe asylum for their cherished faith.

1841.

THE DEATH OF JACOB.

'TWAS noon in Egypt, and the scorching sun
    Poured down his sultry heat on Jacob's tent; —
No noise disturbed the holy calm around,
Save when at times the buzzing harvest-fly
Spun his long note, or far-off bleat of flocks
Came slowly stealing through the burning air.
The feeble breeze was scarcely heard to stir
The ancient palm that stood beside the door;
And the sweet flowers, that to the morning smiled,
Hung down their heads and closed their drooping leaves.
The flocks and shepherds sought a refuge safe,
In cool retreats among the mountain groves.
The fallen sheaves lay withering in the sun,
While the exhausted reapers slept beneath
The spreading branches of the shady trees.
Within the tent where aged Jacob dwelt,
Stood Joseph, and near by two youthful forms,
His sons, Ephraim and Manasseh, who
With weeping eyes looked at the dying sage.
Upon a lowly couch the old man lay,
His long white beard hanging o'er his bosom,

And his feeble eye turned toward heaven.
Raising himself upon his pilgrim-staff,
He lifted up his voice to God, and asked
Of Heaven a blessing for the youthful swains.
His prayer was heard, and like their godly sire,
They lived, and died, in service of the Lord.
The sun went down behind the distant hills,
And his bright beams had scarcely left the skies,
When good old Jacob sank upon his couch.
He died, as all of us might wish to die,
With a firm hope and confidential trust.

1837.

CARLO.

HERE, by his favorite pond, poor Carlo sleeps,
   No more to sport within its waters bright,
Nor more when morning o'er the horizon peeps,
   Shall his glad voice proclaim the early light.

With welcome looks no more will run to greet
   His master, seeking welcome in his eyes,
No more from school, his playmates bound to meet,
   For low in death here honest Carlo lies.

Beneath the branches of this spreading tree,
   With tender care thy friends have made thy grave,
Where often they will come to think of thee,
   And drop a tear for one so good and brave.

1849.

THE OLD SPINNING WHEEL.

THOU ancient wheel, whose gentle song
    Did erewhile please my ear,
When I was joyous, free, and young,
    No longer now I hear:

For in the garret thrust away —
    The prey of worms and rot, —
Far from the genial light of day,
    Thou 'rt doomed to be forgot.

Thou wast my grandam's, and her worth
    Doth make thee dear to me;
Thou wast coeval with her birth —
    Ago a century.

How often, when a wanton boy,
    I 've whirled thee round and round,
And clapped my hands from heartfelt joy,
    At thy inspiring sound!

Those early days are past and gone;
    My childhood's friends have fled;

D

And now that I am sober grown,
　I'd prize thee for the dead.

The flush of youth has left my cheek,
　And manhood's seal is there;
Yet oft in memory I seek
　Those days so void of care.

But fare-thee-well! thou yet mayst lie
　Another space alone,
When to thy nook some friend may hie,
　Long after I am gone.

　1836.

THE AGED MAN.

THAT aged man, that aged man,
　Who slowly totters by my door, —
His life has nearly reached its span, —
　Soon shall we see his form no more.

Once he was young and hale as I,
　His form erect, his footstep true,
And lustre beamed from out his eye,
　Which might have vied with heaven's blue.

Young Jennie was his blooming bride:
　She long beneath the sod hath slept,
And he must soon lie by her side,
　Be unremembered and unwept.

The village knew no comelier pair
　Than in their youth were John and Jane;
Their hearts were light, their prospects fair,
　They were indeed a happy twain.

Their lives an even tenor ran,
　Each day new pleasures brought along,

And at the rise and set of sun,
    Together they would sing a song.

A group of happy children smiled
    Around their ever cheerful hearth,
And every thought of care beguiled,
    With prattle sweet, and constant mirth.

But with the crush of hapless fate,
    This happy group was swept away;
Poor John soon lost his worthy mate,
    And all was sad, that erst was gay.

His children o'er the world now roam,
    Driven by penury's stern hand,
And he is left without a home,
    To wander in his native land.

But though old age has dimmed his eyes,
    And filled his broken heart with pains,
He still has hopes beyond the skies,
    And of his hardship ne'er complains.

1836.

TO CAURUS.

A Y ! blow, thou raging blast !
    And vent thy utmost rage :
Thou canst not forever last :
    Who would thy wrath assuage ?

Thou mak'st the forests bend,
    The mighty ocean roar,
Great oaks thou oft dost rend,
    And shak'st the strongest tower.

All this thou dost, great wind !
    And oftentimes much more ;
But thou thyself art blind ;
    One sways ye by His power,
Whose ever steady hand
Can make ye move, or stand.

1836.

OUR HARBOR.

IT is, indeed, a fair and beauteous sight,
  To see our waters on a summer day,
When the clear sun outpours his bounteous light,
  And blue waves 'neath his rich effulgence play;
While darting fish disport within the tide,
And, bounding by the light boats, swiftly glide.

And thou, fair gem, bedecked in pleasing green,
  That o'er the scene dost cast a cheering smile,
Who does not love, when all exults in sheen,
  To scan thy beauties, lovely Palmer's Isle;
Or land his shallop on the pebbly shore,
And trace thy walks with lingering footsteps o'er?

Where yon old fortress, crumbling fast away,
  Upheaves to view its weather-beaten form,
'Gainst which the dashing billows cast their spray,
  When the old rocks resound the coming storm,
How oft I 've listened to the sea-bird's call,
When resting 'neath the grass-grown, mouldering wall!

Come here, beneath a clear and summer sky,
　When day's bright car rolls down the golden west,
And dwell upon the scenes that meet thy eye,
　While pleased emotions fill thy swelling breast;
For rarely shall a fairer sight be found,
Than such as will thy ardent gaze surround.

If to the west thou turn'st thy raptured eyes,
　A view presents, that may with any vie,
Where our fair town in quiet beauty lies,
　In fair repose beneath the cloudless sky;
While to the east, her younger sister queen,
With her neat roofs and village spire, is seen.

And when, returning from the foaming sea,
　Some fair ship, laden with her oily store,
Breaks on the sight, her loosened sails all free,
　And bends her course towards our happy shore,
How gladly meet these scenes the seaman's eye,
As from the giddy mast he shouts for joy!

　　1837.

MOUNT AUBURN.

HERE I will rest, upon this hillside fair,
   And muse upon the scene that me surrounds,
Where towering oaks keep out the mid-day glare,
   From whose broad tops come forth sweet mellow
      sounds,
   Like funeral chants o'er these sepulchral mounds.
I am alone, and I would wish it so,
   For with high interest the spot abounds ;
And while my soul with solemn thoughts doth glow,
I would a lesson learn, ere to the world I go.

It is the hush of Autumn's genial tide ;
   Far in the west the sun his course hath spent,
And wild clouds in the northern circuit ride,
   While scarce a ray to light my path is lent.
   'T is true, I come no lost friend to lament,
Yet I 've a tear to lend for those who mourn ;
   And even now my rising sighs are spent,
As towards yon grave with musing steps I turn,
Where virtue lies reposed beneath the voiceless urn.

Fair is the spot, and bright in memory's page
    Comes up the day, when bidding books farewell,
With tripping steps I came to hear the sage
    Whose silver voice arose from yonder dell,
    While listening crowds upon his accents dwell.
It was a beauteous day, the morning sun
    Walked in rich splendor up the ambient sky ;
And when adown the western arc he won,
Each haunt of this fair wood glowed with his brilliancy.

But ah, how changed ! this lovely spot then seemed
    Like opening Paradise to my young heart,
For Nature here in rich luxuriance teemed,
    Where monuments now rise of vying art.
    O ! why should pride in this still spot have part?
Rather let Nature in her wildness live ;
    She will around a holy awe impart,
From whence the soul much goodness can derive,
And feel its lagging powers again in life revive.

The evening shades are quickly closing round,
    And every songster to his seat now hies,
While all is hushed throughout this sacred ground,
    Save when from yonder mart low sounds arise,
    That lull the ear like gentle melodies.

D2

And now with pain I bid these scenes farewell,
  Where many a noble form in quiet lies :
Ere I shall come again, ah ! who can tell
Where now may linger they who in this spot shall dwell?

Oct., 1837.

TO * * * *

I SAW thee when thou wast a child, —
  I see thee now to woman grown ;
Yet still that look, so sweet, so mild,
  Remains peculiarly thy own, —
That step the same, so light, so true,
  That form so sylphlike in its grace, —
Thy gentle eye, nor black, nor blue,
  Still lights as erst thy lovely face.

THE OLD TRAMMEL.

RUDE relic of a day long past and gone,
   I deem thee not unworthy of my page,
Thou who erewhile unto our shores wast borne,
   And hast survived to this our modern age.

How many scenes have marked the rolling earth
   Since thou wast first enthralled by tyrant man!
How many years of sadness and of mirth
   Since thy eventful history began!

Alas! where is the hand that fashioned thee,
   Or that which drew thee from the yielding earth?
Long have they been commingled with the dust,
   Yet thou art here, as fresh as at thy birth.

Think not, I pray! from thy neglected state,
   That thou art reckoned but with worthless things;
To me, at least, thy ancient form and date
   A mystic store of pleasant musing brings.

Thou tell'st me of old England's jovial days,
   Which bards in loyal strains would proudly bless,

What time was quaffed the far-famed Wassail Bard ;
  Those roystering days, the days of " good Queen
    Bess," —

When oft within the old ancestral hall
  Loud songs of mirth arose at midnight hour,
While spectres floated round the abbey wall,
  Or witches danced within the crumbling tower, —

When brightly blazed aloft the great yule-clog,
  Of welcome merry Christmas' far-timed fame,
While old and young together daily danced
  With noisy glee around the cheerful flame.

'T is said thou graced'st a parson's kitchen once,
  Who dwelt at ease by Avon's sacred tide,
Where the great Bard first drew his mortal breath,
  Who long hath been the Drama's greatest pride.

Strange sights thou there must oftentimes have seen,
  In those famed days of kitchen romp and glee, .
And often here at eventide, I ween,
  Would " Willy Shakespeare " steal, the maid to see.

But thou wast doomed to leave that happy shore,
  Far o'er the tossing billows to be borne,

And here amid the forest's constant roar
   Be placed, alone thy hapless fate to mourn.

Yet thou, perchance, in some far distant age,
   When ancient worth its due shall meet again,
Wilt from thy hiding-place in pride be borne,
   To shine as erst, thou veteran of the crane!

   1838.

THE OLD SPANISH BELL.

WELCOME, old Bell! to this our busy town,
   Where no rude hand again shall mar thy peace;
For thou with age hast quite revered grown,
   And gladly we thy durance vile release.

Thou cam'st, as story goes, from sunny Spain,
   The land of warrior fame and knightly song,
Where bloody feud, with ever ruthless chain,
   Hath firmly bound the god of Freedom long:

Or else how fair that bright and balmy land!
   With charms profuse, and rich with orange groves,
Through which the stealing zephyrs, cool and bland,
   Make a sweet haunt for age, or youthful loves.

Yet proud old Spain the youthful spirit warms:
   Her border tales of rich and wild romance,
When mailed knights, in rude but glittering arms,
   O'er tented fields led on the bold advance, —

When Moor and Christian long in contest vied,
   Ere war, as now, had gained such subtle art, —

Where many a noble form hath early died ;
    These are enough to stir the dullest heart.

And now, though ancient strife its warning gives,
    Still cruel warfare wastes her pleasant vales,
And the fierce love of feudal contest lives,
    That every haunt of quietude assails.

But far from these, old Bell, thou art removed,
    And much more worthy is thy present state,
Since thy own land to thee hath faithless proved,
    And with foul hands thy rest dared violate.

No cowled monk again shall hear thee ring,
    No trembling nun by thee to vespers hie,
Nor matin peal from thee resume its wing,
    When brisk Aurora mounts the eastern sky.

Thanks unto him whose ever liberal hand
    Hath placed thee on yon stately Gothic tower,
Where the fair moon looks down with visage bland,
    And softly falls the light at sunset hour.

There mayst thou rest, from rude invasion free,
    And sweetly send thy silver notes abroad ;
There loudly ring our nation's jubilee,
    And tell the sacred hour of serving God.
      1838.

DAILY TROUBLES.

———

" These little things are great to little man."

GOLDSMITH.

———

THERE are some trials of a kind
  That vex poor mortal man,
At which though fain he would be blind,
  He rarely ever can :
They come in such a mystic shape,
  Amid the very air,
In vain we strive them to escape ;
  They meet us everywhere.

I mean the daily wars that all
  Have, more or less, to wage,
And which, how-much-soe'er he would,
  No mortal can assuage.
We tell our sorrows to our friend,
  If we have such to call ;
We find it is the same with him,
  And so it is with all.

Your tailor makes your coat too tight,
  Your pantaloons too small,

And where you look for warmth and ease,
  You find yourself in thrall;
He swears it is a splendid fit,
  And winks upon the sly,
While you in vain try to convince
  Him of your agony.

Old Crispin, he abuses you,
  Although an honest wretch,
And when you say your boots are snug,
  He quick replies, "They'll stretch";
Or if, perhaps, they are too large,
  You tell him thus you think,
He's ready for you here again,
  And says, "They soon will shrink."

Your grocer sends you home some tea,
  "The very best of tea";
You are a blockhead if you dare
  With him to disagree.
And when to each we e'er complain,
  As we are apt to do,
They say, "We can all others suit,
  Except, sir, it is you."

In vain we would the precept urge,
  As through the world we pass,

The lesson of the golden mean,
  " In medio veritas."
And so we 're doomed to jog along,
  Through this life's thorny road,
And take our lot from day to day,
  Still hoping for the good.

1838.

FAREWELL.

TO H. W. L.

FAREWELL! no more together shall we tread
    Our long frequented paths through woods and
      fields,
Where we so oft, by genial spirits led,
    Have felt the boon that Nature kindly yields.
But not forgotten shall our friendship be;
    Begun in youth, O! may it last with age,
And when alone I wander far from thee,
    I 'll oft revert to memory's hallowed page.

1838.

SIMPLICITY.

CHILDLIKE Simplicity, thou Heaven-born maid!
 Sweet is the influence that pervades thy walks;
Gentle and unobtrusive, thou dost dwell
In quiet vales, far from vain Fashion's mart.
Thou shunn'st the least approach of worldliness,
And mak'st thy home within the pure of heart.
Such is the stillness of this sacred spot,
Where Nature undisturbed lends her fair charm,
I seem to see thee in thy virgin robes
Of purest white, whose graceful folds
But half conceal thy form of classic grace,
As thou along some cooling woodland shade
Dost glide, making its echoes to rejoice;
Thy silken hair in careless beauty spread,
And tossed beneath the stealing zephyr's touch.
After thy gentle step bright flowers arise
And fill the air with fragrance. Thou shunn'st not
The homes of rural industry, where blooming Health,
Thy twin-born sister, dwells in kindred grace.
And here, within this unadorned fane,
Where silence, monitor to erring man,

Broods like a gentle dove, 't is sweet to find thee.
How deep the quiet of this solemn hour!
Made solemn by the Spirit's holy calm,
Where from all noise, all strife, all earthly things,
While the rude world without is bustling on,
Retired within the temple of the heart,
These few and humble worshippers of God
Assemble in their neat and sober guise.
And they are thankful that they thus can come,
And humbly worship in their simple way,
At the eternal shrine of holiness.
No wars, no persecutions, now appear,
Such as erewhile disturbed their peaceful ranks.
O! suffering bitter, persecution rare,
Were once inflicted on these faithful souls,
Who calmly bore them all for conscience' sake.
If thou wouldst love them, read the works of Fox,
Of Barclay, Sewell, and of noble Penn,
And others whom the Holy Spirit led
Through conflicts hard, and tribulations deep.
Here meditation well may enter free,
And does she not?　Look on those earnest brows,
And say if vacancy be found within.
No pomp, no show, nor pride of worship here;
No " pealing anthem swells the note of praise,"

Nor costly trappings lure the wandering eye.
Methinks 't is well, this waiting on our Lord,
This simple worship of the Heavenly King.
Hear'st thou that voice, so gentle in its tone,
Those words so simple, yet with meaning fraught,
That from the heart moved by the Spirit come?
No show of language marks the peaceful truths;
No tropes or figures rattle from the tongue,
Such as too oft set forth the schoolman's page,
Laboring to prove some vexed doctrine's point,
Which, when 't is done, none may the wiser be, —
Cobwebs that tie the energies of soul,
And bind it down to earth, when it should soar
To realms above, where the pure Spirit reigns.
Why will poor man thus shackle his weak steps,
And limp in darkness to the yawning grave?
O! shake it off; and like the viper's fang
Abhor its poison, that engenders death.
All, all is plain, where true religion's found;
The simplest soul that lives may understand:
Such is the teaching of the Friend of man.
Is God exalted by man's artifice?
Can proud cathedral, with its swelling dome,
Or organ rolling thunder 'neath its roof,
Give the Almighty pleasure?   Vain, foolish man!

To think in these that thou shalt hasten bliss.
God seeks the humble and devoted heart —
All else is dross, unworthy of least note;
For when the soul would hold communion deep,
And feel the presence of the living God,
How welcome silence, fosterer of thought!
What fitter place than quiet haunt like this
To rest awhile, and dwell on life and death,
On Man's formation, mystery profound!
The wisdom of his God, past finding out,
His bounteous grace, his tender guardian care;
Peace to the soul it brings, and solid good?
When thy worn spirit sinks beneath its load,
When the proud world scoffs at thy humble walk,
When thou are pained, and almost tired of life,
When friends break troth, or those thou hast esteemed
Of worth beyond compare are called away,
Then seek the silent sitting of the Friends,
And feel its gentle influence on thy soul.

1839.

AUTUMN DAYS.

THESE Autumn days, how gloriously they come!
    A welcome train, though clad in sober guise,
For with them come the mellowing tints of life,
Borne to the soul from every scene around :
The influence fills the grove, the upland lawn,
And each fair haunt that Nature daily gilds.
There is beauty in the Spring-tide year,
When the first freshness of the fields comes on,
And the sweet carols of the woodland choir
Are heard from every tree and hedge around,
Charming the ear with their delightful notes.
There, too, is richness in fair Summer's time,
When the sweet perfume of the gentle flowers
Fills the wide air, and, borne along the breeze,
Comes with delight upon the freshened sense.
But, like a sage with honors bending low,
Brown Autumn moves sedately o'er the earth.
Scenes that of late flashed in the noontide beam,
And sent a fragrance round their still retreats,
In sober livery now waiting stand,
Ere the keen frosts shall nip their latest charms.

How dear this time to him who loves to stray
Far in the woods to meditate alone :
The quickening spirit that lights up the soul
Hath here a power that rarely else is found,
A soothing charm, that prompts the soul to good.
The little bird, that hops from spray to spray,
Uttering his gentle note of happiness,
And the loud jay, that now is often heard,
Perched high on some old monarch of the woods,
Or solemn crow, bending his distant way
Along the woodland skirt to join his mates,
Welcome the wanderer to their happy realms.
Beware, ye sportsmen, who with murderous hearts
Seek the sweet lives that gladden these abodes !
Your deadly sounds no music have for me,
Though often sung in songs of cheering rhyme.
Cease your mad sports, and think upon yourselves ;
Dwell for a moment on the worth of life ;
Think how much happiness you can destroy
By one foul aim, and then abhor the deed.
Here, too, the rabbit, and the timorous hare,
The whirring partridge, and the gentle quail,
And thou, sweet harbinger of pleasing thought,
That lend'st thy song to charm the musing hour,
Thou little cricket ! dear to childhood's days, —

In every spot at this rich Autumn time
Thou find'st a home, a welcome home, I ween;
Welcome to me thou art, for thou dost tell
Of happy hours in days long fled away,
When boyhood's fancy dreamed of unbought joys,
And aspiration filled my youthful heart.
Then like a boon our Indian Summer comes,
Among the glooms sweet Summer's death hath left.
O! if there be on earth a season given,
When the calm influence of a heavenly scene
To mortals is allowed, it must be this,
So like our dreams of bliss its spirit seems.
How gladly to the sick man's room it comes,
When from his cot he trembling ventures forth
To catch the fragrance of the genial breeze!
While all around admonishes of death. ·
Sweet breezes blow o'er Italy's fair soil,
And balmy air is breathed in Holy land;
The isles of Greece are fanned by odorous gales;
Old England, too, her charms profusely spreads,
Hoary with time, and filled with rich romance;
But these in charms supreme might fain compare
With our own land when Indian Summer reigns.
O! if the soul can aught receive of life
From outward sense, it must be at this time,

E

When Nature in her solemn stole is clad,
Breathing a moral to the wakened heart.
Lover of pleasure, leave all guilty sports,
And wander forth mid Nature's scenes awhile,
At this rich season of the waning year.
Here thou wilt find naught to disturb thy soul,
No strife to bid the wounded spirit rise ;
Here learn the lesson which true wisdom gives,
That God alone the anxious heart can soothe,
And that in Him thou shouldst repose thy trust.
How the wide air around doth teem with joy !
And even the insects that have dormant lain
Within the nooks and crevices of the earth,
Now venture forth again to taste of life,
While in the woods the sprightly black-cap tunes
His lonely whistle from some slender bough,
Which, borne along the health-inspiring breeze,
Sounds like a mellow dirge to Summer's reign.

    Oct., 1839.

THE GOTHIC TOWER.

SEEN through the trees, I love to view
    Yon church's gothic tower,
In Summer time when skies are blue,
    But most at sunset hour :

For then, lit up by those bright hues
    Which deck the close of day,
No sight more richly could combine
    The solemn and the gay.

I love, too, in chill Winter's reign,
    When all things feel his doom,
To gaze upon its stately form,
    Amid surrounding gloom.

And now, half hid with falling snow,
    Like frosty head of age,
Its charms, seen through the misty veil,
    My musings still engage :

My thoughts are borne far o'er the sea,
    To Britain's glorious shore,
And there, through scenes of ancient days,
    Her storied haunts explore ; —

I seem to see some village church,
　　Built long, long time ago,
With ivy clad, and brown with age,
　　From whence rich memories flow ;

Within its solemn aisles alone,
　　With awe I slowly tread,
For on its sacred walls appear
　　The emblems of the dead ;

From out whose quaint and crumbling tower,
　　Where hangs the time-worn bell,
With busy fancy rapt I hear
　　The curfew's warning knell ;

Or borne along the rural lane,
　　A tale most sad to tell,
With pious awe I list, while tolls
　　The mournful passing bell.

Such thoughts at times my musings fill,
　　When at my window seated,
For there, oft seen through yonder trees,
　　That tower my eyes hath greeted.

　　　1839.

SIMPLICITY.

I 'M smitten of Simplicity,
    That gentle maid with downcast eye,
Unheeded by the passer-by,
For whom she lends a heartfelt sigh.
Kind solacer of earthly ills,
With balm the heart thy spirit fills,
When grief and troubles thick surround,
And bow us weeping to the ground.
Not mid the sordid ranks of man
Shall we thy smiling features scan,
Where Folly, in her bauble car,
Wields her sceptre wide and far, —
Where grasping Gain bestrides the land,
With vassals ready at his hand,
Who bow unto his iron shrine
As though he were a God divine :
But in the quiet walks of life,
Far from all calumny and strife,
Where simple Truth in beauty lies,
We find thy gentle sympathies.

1839.

THE LOSS OF THE LEXINGTON.

WHAT muse can paint the horrors of that night?
    What fancy sketch that last, that fatal hour?
Alas! the sickened heart turns with affright,
    And shuddering, contemplates the God of power.

Roused from their slumbers, or from happy dreams
    Of home and welcome from beloved friends,
The awful sight at once upon them beams,
    And to their hearts its rending sorrow sends.

And when the last, though lingering hope had fled,
    And consciousness of their sad fate had come,
When soon their names should rest among the dead,
    And mourning fill the late fair, happy home:

O! then assembled on the burning deck,
    Father and mother, child and reverend sage,
No hand the raging element to check,
    What thoughts their souls must that dread hour engage!

O! Thou who rul'st in Heavenly realms above,
    Who guidest the winged lightning in its speed,

Thou who art ever crowned the God of love,
  Who hast our sinful souls from thraldom freed, —

O ! to our weak, though anguished hearts declare
  The secret of thy mighty Providence ;
List to the yearnings of our inmost prayer,
  And fill with sacred light our inmost sense.

But why, O soul, such mysteries seek to know?
  Why for a moment search His sovereign light?
Rather in faith to His omniscience bow,
  Trusting in Him : whate'er He does is right.

Jan. 19th, 1840.

THE POET SOUTHEY:

ON LEARNING THAT HIS MIND HAD FAILED FROM OVER EXERTION.

MY heart is sad, that one so much beloved
By every friend of pure and lofty verse,
That he, the high-toned bard, should thus be doomed,
One whose noble mind beamed so much truth,
And sent a radiance throughout every land,
Who, from the labors of his busy pen,
Has drawn around him those of high renown,
As strong, admiring friends, and raised amid
Those beauteous lakes an interest rich and rare ; —
'T is sad indeed to dwell upon his lot.
No more, as erst, shall wake his tuneful lyre ;
Quenched is that ardor which adorned his youth,
While, musing 'neath old Oxford's classic shades,
He sung of Nature in her fair retreats.
As on thy face, which from the artist's hand
Hath crossed the Atlantic wave and reached me here,
I gaze, its spirit seems to mark thy fate.
O gentle poet ! — thee I gentle call,
For thou possess'st a heart most keenly strung

To all the kindlier pulses of the soul, —
Thou hast, dear bard, loved well fair Nature's court,
And long hast practiced in her genial cause.
Methinks I see thee now, wandering alone
Among the woods and streams of thy own home,
Where old Helvellyn lifts his hoary head
Within fair Keswick's solitary vale,
Muttering some half-lost lay of childhood's hour;
A tear upon thy eye, thy soul suffused
With childish fancies, long forgotten friends
Flitting like spirits through thy wildered mind,
Remembering better scenes of early days
Than those more recent.   Such, alas! too true.
But wherefore mourn his lot? the all-seeing Eye
Beholds and guards him, and will ne'er forsake
One in whom virtue ever found a friend;
One who could raise his strong, impassioned verse
To Him who smiled upon his infant face.
And while old England's clarion voice is heard
Among the nations of the wide-spread earth,
The name of Southey shall a watchword be
To the young minstrel musing on his page:
The name of Southey shall be dear to all.

1841.

E2

THE NIGHT WIND.

WIND, that against my casement beatest,
    As if thou wouldst come in, despite of checks,
Wherefore thy rage and roar? art thou abroad
This wild and darksome night, whoe'er thou meetest
To battle with thy harsh and ruthless wand?
Thou shak'st the dwellings of the shivering poor,
And speed'st the wight who hastens onward home;
Thou bellowest down the lofty chimney's throat,
And shock'st the group around the blazing hearth;
Thou bowest the forest in thy furious course,
And scatterest fragments of their mighty arms; —
These and far more, thy terrors on the land:
But on old ocean's deep and boundless waste
Thou spend'st thy fury; navies thou dost sweep
Like winnowed chaff, and on the rocky shores
Scatterest around the huge and groaning hulks,
And all throughout their torn and thrashing canvas
Thou howlest like a raging beast of prey.
Old towers and beacons on promontories
Shake fearfully, and extend forth in vain
The guidance that but for thee were welcome;

Now only showing, with too fatal truth,
As the huge billows leave the foaming shore,
The rocks' deep channels, threatening instant doom
To the poor seaman clinging to some plank
Or scattered fragment of the gallant bark.
But morn shall come again, and thou thy rage
Shalt lose ; the cheerful sun shall usher in
The day, and all around will smile again.

TRUE HEROISM.

SUGGESTED BY THE NOBLE ACT OF A GENTLEMAN, IN SAVING
THE LIFE OF A DROWNING BOY AT THE EXTREME PERIL
OF HIS OWN.

TEARS fill the eye from nature's strong emotion,
  The heart beats quicker, almost unto pain,
And feelings kin to spiritual devotion
  Wake from their slumberous state to life again.

Ah! noble truly was that high-born action;
  Rather from heaven than earth such deeds must spring;
Vain shall the muse, or praise with its attraction,
  Strive on such merit their reward to bring.

How in the distance shrinks the vast collection
  Of deeds that men call great, but born of earth!
Cast to the winds the sordid, rank infection
  That thrusts itself before such peerless worth!

Blush ye! who, ruled by this world's vain ambition,
  In your own circumscribed sphere would shine, —
Seeker for wealth, or heartless politician,
  Who sacrifice alone at Mammon's shrine.

Come, man of war, in deeds of blood victorious,
    Whose dreadful trade the erring world calls brave ;
Come, learn from this how much more truly glorious
    It is one human being's life to save.

Amid the heartlessness and fierce commotion
    With which the earth throughout her bounds is filled,
The soul is cheered at such sublime devotion,
    And with new vigor every nerve is thrilled.

Wide through the land let such blessed deeds be sounded ;
    Let Virtue lift her head to wear the crown,
And selfishness, with its proud claims confounded,
    From all the wise and good receive a frown.

Enough for him, howe'er, the approbation
    That heaven grants to such transcendent worth, —
Supremely more than if a mighty nation
    Its praise in one loud chorus shouted forth.

THE FATHER'S LAMENT.

I WATCHED him with a father's care;
  He was my only son, and pride;
His name was ever in my prayer,
  But ah! my poor boy died.

His mother smoothed his cold, pale brow,
  And looked, nor spoke, but sighed:
Alas! I seem to see him now,
  But O! my poor boy died.

We laid him in his lonely grave,
  Beside the greenwood tree,
Whose branches o'er him softly wave,
  And breezes murmur free.

I seem to see his cherub face,
  As when a little child,
And strive each precious charm to trace,
  My sorrow to beguile.

But ah! fond memory seeks in vain,
  Our darling hope to find;
The search but gives a greater pain,
  And sadder leaves the mind.

DAYBREAK.

FAINT streaks of day now paint the ambient skies,
  While all is still through the wide welkin round,
Save the low voice of varied harmonies,
  That fills the morning air with gentle sound ;

Or when at times the early cocks rejoice,
  To welcome in the brisk returning day ;
Or far away some distant watch-dog's voice,
  That greets the early traveller on his way.

'T is pleasant in this fresh and quiet hour
  To wander forth, fair Nature's works among,
And learn from her the great Creator's power,
  Ere all her varied haunts break forth in song.

Not yet is heard the busy hum of man,
  That soon shall wake when Sol resumes his car ;
The noise of wheels, and laboring artisan,
  Resounding from the noisy mart afar.

THE POET'S WEALTH.

'TIS not the costly pearl or burnished gold,
   Nor stately equipage and titled name,
That to the Poet's heart fresh charms unfold,
   And breathe into his soul that quenchless flame;
   Nor does he long their fleeting toys to claim;
His soul o'erleaps such transitory things,
   And soars above to Him from whence they came;
Or with delight to Truth's fair temple clings,
And of her heavenly birth with rapture ever sings.

He looks abroad through Nature's vast domain,
   Forever teeming with attractions dear,
The shady woodland, and the outstretched plain,
   To his rapt soul with mystic charms appear,
   And fill his glowing mind with welcome cheer.
What though the heartless crowd may on him frown,
   And seek his honest fame to waste or blear?
In vain they strive the spirit to keep down
Of heavenly birth: fair Virtue holds the crown.

SEASIDE.

DARK, dropping clouds are rolling overhead;
  The sea drives wildly o'er these craggy rocks,
Whose booming mingles with the sea-bird's cry;
While seated here within this cavern dark,
My mind is filled with awe and solemn thought.
In the dim distance, on the horizon's edge,
A bark is moving on her distant voyage,
And there upon her deck is human life;
The night is near, with tempest in her shroud,
And that fair ship must bide the raging storm:
May He who holds the waters in His hand
Guide her in safety to her destined port.
O! who can sit him down on this dread spot
In such an hour as this, and not be filled
With admiration for the Mighty One,
Who piled in such bold heaps these ponderous rocks?
I thank thee with no Pharisaic pride,
My God, that I am not of that cold class
Whom the vain glitter of the world so charms,
That mid thy most exalted works forget
The great Framer of them; but by thy grace
Can feel indeed thou shouldst be remembered,
And, too, with filial reverence, deep and full.

WILD FLOWERS.

YE gentle children of the woods and fields,
  I love to wander through your quiet haunts,
While all around a healthful fragrance yields,
  And the sweet thrush his mellow carol chants:

For in your ever fair and peaceful homes,
  Naught of the world's ungenerous strife is found,
But gladness to the weary spirit comes,
  And fills the scene with happiness around.

Then let me often seek the greenwood shade,
  Or trace the path across the meadow green,
When Spring's sweet warblers sing through wood and
      glade,
  Or Summer flowers enliven all the scene.

INSECT HARMONY.

O MUCH to me, in hours of pain or grief,
    The simple melody of insect life !
A soothing quiet rests upon my mind,
While gently on my ear their chant is heard ;
The memory of past and sunnier days,
When life was fresher, and when hope was strong,
Passes in pleasing view before my mind ;
The fields of life, that once such promise gave,
Ere the sharp scythe of time had mown them down,
Present again their flowers and verdant crops,
Seen through the vista of departed years.
Sweet, gentle sounds, to him with ear attuned
By sorrow, or the Spirit's holier calm, —
The humble, contemplative mind,
That shuns the discords of the jarring crowd,
And seeks in quiet for its purer joys !

OLD JOY.

THOUGH marks of age, old honest Joy,
    Are gathering fast on thee,
Thou still dost love the eager chase
    O'er hill-top and o'er lea.

And when thy master takes his gun
    To seek the whirring quail,
All ready still to join the sport,
    Thou bark'st and wagg'st thy tail.

But what to me endears thee more, —
    Thy kind and gentle heart,
Thy cheerful welcome unto all,
    Thy sad looks when we part.

But soon poor Joy must pass away, —
    I pray with little pain;
For rarely on this earth may we
    Behold his like again.

THE STRICKEN DEER.

A Y ! pass her by, and cast a scornful look,
    Nor deign to speak to one so lowly crushed!
Let low-born calumny, and scandal base,
Do their whole work, nor grant a friendly check.
Ah ! gentle lady, listen : time has been
When not so ye would have passed each other ;
A time when that sad face was lighted up
With radiant beauty that had few compeers ;
When on that cheek, now pale and wan, sat smiles
To welcome all ; — and she was loved by all.
It matters not to me if she has fallen, —
Fallen indeed by calumny's red hand !
Shall we, already loaded with our own deep sins,
  Sins known, perhaps, but to God and ourselves,
Pretend to judge, and to make outcast one
Whose cruel lot, had it been ours to bear,
We might have merited by our misdeeds.
If He who taught us all things good while here,
Could pardon, and declare, " Go, sin no more,"
Shall we poor pensioners pretend to scorn
A bereaved and broken fellow-creature, whom

The Lord in his kind mercy hath forgiven?
For one, I gladly give to such my hand,
And gentlest words, to cheer her on her way,
For lone and weary is her pilgrimage.

THE POETASTER.

THE bard who does not rise above
    The low and commonplace of life,
Whose highest efforts only prove
A level with his daily strife,
But slender title to the name
Of poet, or of seer, can claim :—
His lines may flow in mellow verse,
His periods rounded off, and terse ;
But wanting Nature's magic grace,
A few short years shall all efface.

THE LAST OF THE WAMPANOAGS.

SAD and alone the warrior sank him down,
　　Beneath the branches of a riven oak;
Like leaves before the Autumn blast had flown
　　His once brave comrades, by the white man's stroke.

He looked upon the ancient forest trees,
　　Within whose fostering shade his fathers slept;
And as their tops waved to the passing breeze,
　　He sighed adieu, and though a savage, wept.

His bow unstrung, his hatchet cast aside,
　　His war-plumes vainly placed upon his brow,
His manly breast no longer swelled with pride,
　　But doomed, alas! beneath his fate to bow, —

His heart is broken, and from death alone
　　He seeks a refuge, where he may again,
In broader fields, and hunting-grounds unknown,
　　Meet his lost race, no more to suffer pain.

So stretched upon the mossy woodland turf,
　　He wraps his robe around his heaving breast;

The brown November leaves upon him fall,
   And here alone he finds a final rest.

The moaning winds throughout the forest drear,
   A fitting requiem for the warrior lend,
Unheard by him, for death has sealed his ear,
   And all his sorrows there have found an end.

HAUGHTINESS.

BEAUTIFUL! despite her scorn and pride,
   But ah! more beauteous still,
If these base faults were cast aside,
   That so much goodness kill.

How sad, where so much virtue strives
   To conquer every sin,
That native haughtiness survives,
   Too oft the prize to win!

WINTER THOUGHTS.

WHEN the Winter wind is blowing
  Round our dwellings sharp and clear,
And the cheerful hearth is glowing
  With its warm and steady cheer,
Think ye then of those who languish
  In some lone and cheerless shed,
Whence, to swell the soul with anguish,
  All their former hopes are fled.

Where the widow in her sorrow
  Shivers in her cold, dull room,
Looking for the hopeless morrow,
  But to lengthen out her gloom,—
Late at night you there will find her,
  Plying at her lonely task;
Thoughts of other days attend her,
  But of her who now shall ask?

Stretched upon his humble pallet,
  Pale and weak, the poor man lies;
Anxious still, his heart is yearning
  For those bound by dearest ties.

F

Gentle forms are suffering near us,
  Those who better days have known,
Sad misfortune's hapless children,
  Left upon the world alone.

These are no wrought tales of fiction,
  That the feeling tear may flow;
Fancy's forms, or labored diction,
  Little suit the tale of woe.
Stern the hand of want is pressing,
  On the victims of his sway,
Tyrant-like each hope possessing,
  That might smooth their weary way.

1843.

LINES TO S. S.

HOW sweet the voice of Truth, when from the lips
    Of those whom the pure Spirit moves in love!
O! ever sweet the voice of woman's love;
But never more than when in the great cause
Of Christian truth engaged: ah, then indeed
Its gentle tones awake the inmost soul,
And rouse its energies to Heavenly things.
The cares of life, the world with all its wiles,
Are borne away, and a calm, thoughtful mood
Spreads o'er the mind, till the whole soul
Is held in high communion with the God of all.
So hath my soul been moved by thy kind words,
O gentle woman; and to thee my heart
Would bear its better feelings, and for thee
Desire the best of blessings from our Father's hand.
O, when temptations from the world surround,
When struggling with the adverse tide of sin,
Or when deep sorrow shall come o'er my path,
May I then think of thy kind, loving words,
And learn of thee to look to Him above,
Who giveth balm to heal the wounded heart.

1843.

THE MAIDEN'S LAMENT.

MY thoughts are very sad to-night —
    My heart is very sad,
For I've been thinking of the days
    When my young heart was glad, —

When oft within my father's hall
    The merry dance went round,
And kindly voices greeted me
    With their familiar sound.

I call to mind my noble sire,
    My mother's lovely face :
Whose cherished smile from this poor heart,
    No time will e'er efface.

How happy then we rambled o'er
    Our own extensive grounds,
My father with his merry friends,
    His horses and his hounds !

The dew-drop hung upon the rose
    That reached my window high ;

While blithely on the aged yew
The red-breast warbled nigh.

But O! those happy days have fled,
And I am left alone :
The world but little cares for rank,
When once its wealth is gone.

1843.

THE ANEMONE.

—

TO E. S. A.

—

I KNOW a gentle flower that blows,
    When Winter's chilling winds have fled,
And, loth its beauty to disclose,
    It often hides its modest head.

The careless eye may not perceive
    This lowly flower, so sweet and fair;
For me, howe'er, in wood or field,
    No sweeter scents the morning air.

I meet it on my favorite walk,
    And stop to view its simple charms,
As, bending on its slender stalk,
    It trusts to Nature's kindly arms.

This gentle flower, whose modest grace
    So often hath delighted me,
Though missed mid Summer's gayer race,
    I have compared, dear child, to thee.

1843.

WILLIAM LLOYD GARRISON.

BRAVE Spirit! the great multitude of men
But little comprehend thee — whether they
Who congregate upon the busy mart
Of commerce, or in halls of classic lore,
Or they whose names stand high upon the scroll
Of the Republic, if so may be called
That which makes lawful trade in human flesh!
These little know the greatness of thy soul,
Thou more than noble, follower of the Truth!
They, each and all, however high their aims,
However praised in patriotic strains,
Have something — much of worldly enterprise.
The gifts and plaudits of their fellow-men
Attend them, and cheer on their daily course;
But thou, thou of the soul sublime! who hast
Spent thy early manhood, and even now,
In thy mature and much experienced life,
Art still unceasing in thy arduous toil,
To break the shackles from thy brothers' limbs,
Whose groans so long have sounded in thy heart.
Thou art despised, and scoffed at by the proud,

And mighty, — prices set upon thy head,
As if thou were a cut-throat, or a knave.
This is, however, but the same story
The world has ever told against the good :
Man is too slow to learn ; his stubborn will
Confronts his reason, and shipwrecks the soul.
That which is plain, so plain that all may see,
The equal rights of every human soul,
To the best gifts of Providence divine,
The just and equal sway of human power,
As delegated from the Heavenly King,
Are truths but little heeded ; but instead,
A blind, and headstrong, passion takes the lead, —
Or else, how in a land boasting so much
Of liberty, and equal rights for all,
How comes it that not all who till the ground
Are left to enjoy the fruit of their hard toil,
But wear the name of slave? slave ! in a land
Called Christian ! claiming to be first of all
The nations that spread o'er the globe,
In the protection of the rights of man.
But, O my country, dearly as I love
The land that gave me, and my fathers, birth,
I blush, when in the sight of other lands,
I contemplate thy sore disgrace, — thou who

Persecutest too, thy sons who nobly strive
To wipe the stain from off thy else fair face.
And he who in these lines I memorize,
In whose large soul oft wake the gentlest throbs,
Who loves his fellow-man wherever found,
Whether on Lapland's cold, and sterile soil,
Where Nova Zembla's icy turrets rise,
Or where the scorching sun of Afric shines.
Is it not strange that he should thus be held!
But not by all art thou despised, my friend, —
Friend of mankind.   I, at least, do claim,
In common with the chosen few who stand
Firm for the bondman's cause, come whate'er may,
To honor, and respect, thy high-born worth.
Thou, too, already rank'st in other lands,
(And soon wilt rank through our own, I ween,)
With the most honored names, whom good men bless.
Fierce, and bitter persecution have beset
The path that Wilberforce, and Clarkson trod :
The one, now gone from works unto rewards,
The other, calmly reaping his just praise.
Thy country, too, in better days, my friend,
Shall gladly pay the tribute due to thee.
But press thou on!   Thou need'st, 't is true,
No word of counsel, or of cheer from me :

F2

Straight is thy course, thy clear, undaunted eye
Knows well the goal, and thy prophetic wand
Is ever ready to point out the way.
Men may pretend to hold thee in contempt,
And make it vulgar to join hands with thee.
'T is but a sham! in truth they honor thee,
Yet want the courage to stand by thy side.
But thou, far-looking, heed'st not praise, nor blame,
Sustained by Him for whose great cause thou liv'st
Year after year, with ne'er untiring zeal,
Still lead'st the van of that small company,
Who yet may save our country from her fall.

1845.

TRUE GREATNESS—THOMAS CLARKSON.

ALL is not greatness that mankind so deem!
  How blind, how dark, the multitudes appear!
Bowing before the standards they have raised.
O! when will man learn he has nobler claims,
Than just to follow in the old worn track
Of base ambition! when will he arise,
And, throwing off the gyves that have so long
Shackled, and burdened, all his high-born aims,
Walk forth in noble independence of the truth!
Not he who gains the plaudits of the crowd,
Who wears the civic crown, and rules in pomp,
Who has the envy of his fellow-men,
Less fortunate considered than himself;
Not he who, on the rostrum of debate,
Can harangue thousands on some trifling theme,
And stir their souls to some unhallowed fire;
These are not great, and live but for the day —
Mere butterflies, that flitter a few hours,
And then are left to perish on the ground.
He who is loyal unto truth alone,
Whom no temptations false can e'er allure,

Who ever loves the good, the right his choice,
Whether it brings him peace or crown of thorns, —
He may be humble, may be noble born,
As man has chosen so to speak of man, —
He, he is true, and he alone is great.
Such, noble Clarkson! was thy virtuous life, —
Happy the country that can claim thy birth,
And well may England cherish thy great name..
Well may the nations claim thee as their own,
Thou more than noble — glorious in the Truth!
When, through the long-drawn years of coming time,
The last faint tinkle of the once loud peal
That swelled the praise of warriors, and of kings,
Shall die upon the ear, to wake no more,
Then shall the chorus of united song
Chant forth the name of him whose chief delight
Was to plant happiness where woe was found, —
Him shall they write, in title bold, and strong,
A Friend of Man; what nobler can be given?

    1846.

SONNET—THOMAS CLARKSON.

DIED ON HIS 87TH BIRTHDAY, SEPT. 26TH, 1846.

AS musingly I trace the historic page,
    Dark with the deeds of tyranny, and blood
  That hurl along whole nations like a flood,
At widened intervals some honored sage
Shines with rich lustre in his darkling age,
    Calling aloud for justice in the land
    Where frowning king, and bloody warrior, stand,
Or with fierce madness their base conflicts wage:
But from the great, and good, the earth has known,
    Than Clarkson, I can find no clearer name.
When to the winds the warrior's fame is flown,
    The nations shall aloud his worth proclaim,
    And gladly celebrate his peerless fame.

1846.

SONNET TO M. W. C.

PRESS on ! still let thy cheering voice go forth !
   Still boldly plead thy fellow-being's right !
Thy soul sustained by Him, the Lord of Might,
Shines with rich lustre in the darkened North :
Far to the South is seen its kindling ray,
   Though little heeded in that tyrant land,
   By those who at their cursed Moloch stand,
Where sullen sits the demon of Dismay !
But there, e'en there, thy spirit tones have sped, —
   The panting Slave thou oft hast made rejoice ;
   And quailing 'neath the justice of thy voice,
The surly Master hath its warning fled.
Press on ! devoted one, thy way is clear ;
Led by the Truth, thy soul has naught to fear.

1846.

LINES

TO THE TRANSATLANTIC FRIENDS OF THE SLAVE.

YE who across the broad Atlantic wave
    Have sent your kindly voices hitherward,
Whilst those who should at our right hand be found
Have recreant proved to Nature, and to Truth,
We gladly hail ye as our cherished friends !
Ye who, afar from such heart-rending scenes
As blot the fair fields of our native land,
Have wept to hear the distant tale of woe ;
Ye, in whose breasts no base-born hate resides ;
Ye, who can look on Afric's sable sons
And call them brethren, heirs of the same rights
That the great Giver of all good designs
For man, wherever found throughout the globe, —
We love to rank ye with the truly great —
The noble benefactors of our race.
Clarkson ! thy life awakens in our souls
The truest reverence due to Love, and Truth :
Our infant lips oft lisped thy revered name,
And with increasing years our love has grown.
And ye, of later date, ye, noble ones,

To whom we owe so much of cheer, and strength,
Your names are watchwords in our sacred cause!
Thompson, thy thrilling tones of eloquence
Not yet have died away upon our ears —
Thy glowing thoughts are treasured in our hearts, —
Bowring, thy gifted pen, so freely lent
To spread the cause of Freedom, and of Truth, —
Houghton, and Webb, so constant at your posts,
Ye clear, and fearless pleaders for the Right!
And Martineau, and Pease, your generous aid
We fondly prize among our choicest gifts.
Abdy, thou too, whose rich and classic claims
Are unsurpassed but by thy feeling heart;
Howitt, than whom no firmer, truer name,
England affords throughout her broad domains;
And Morpeth, nobler in the cause of Truth
Than in thy own illustrious name and rank, —
We love ye all, and, in the bondman's name,
Invoke Heaven's blessings on your noble lives.

1845.

IMPROMPTU.

A MIND determined to be strong,
Must labor hard, and labor long,
Must seek in Nature's wide domain,
The Truth that o'er his heart shall reign, —
Some noble object to engage
His early years, and downward age ;
For Man, without some grand pursuit,
Is little raised above the brute.
If honest in his noble aim,
All selfish end he will disclaim ;
And steering onward for the right,
Will soon discern the beacon light,
That from the ocean waste before,
Shall bring him to some peaceful shore.

1848.

HO! HELP!

GIVE up thy gold, thou man of wealth ;
    Thy strength give us, thou man of health
Stretch forth thy hand, and do thy part ;
Thou who art poor, give us thy heart !
The slave is groaning in his chains ;
His blood has cursed our hills and plains ;
Our foes, regardless of his fate,
Have sadly wrecked " the ship of state " ;
Her mildewed sails droop o'er her side,
Her hull is drifting with the tide :
Ho ! to the helm, some master bold !
Each gallant sailor seize his hold !
Man every yard, let hope prevail,
And to the breeze set every sail ;
No longer stand aside dismayed,
But let your valor be displayed.
Shall that low, black and blood-stained craft,
Which dire tornadoes hither waft,
Our strong and ready crew appall?
Shall they to Slavery's dictates fall?

A manly stand may save us now ;
A shrinking fear must lay us low.
Come from your farms, ye yeomen brave !
Come as your fathers came, to save !
The cause of Liberty demands
A nobler service at your hands ;
Old Nature yielding to your toil
The very incense of her soil,
While every foot of upturned ground
The voice of Freedom swells around.
Come from the workshop, and the mart ;
'T is Liberty that claims your part ;
Not only for the bleeding slave,
But that which all must rouse to save ;
For now within our very homes
The tyrant with his mandate comes.
Ho ! to the rescue, sons, and sires !
Arouse your strong ancestral fires !

1850.

THE FIELD.

I SEE a field before my view,
   The harvest bending to the gale;
The laborers in that field are few,
   But hearts who ne'er in duty fail.

I 'd rather labor with that band,
   A humble gleaner though it be,
Than feast within the Southron's land,
   Bedecked with spoils of slavery, —

Than sit in legislative hall,
   The champion of its council board,
While listening as my accents fall,
   The heartless crowd my words should hoard, —

Than roam the world, its sights to see,
   Or gather gold in coffers deep, —
Than have my name in blazonry,
   For which some human heart might weep.

The towering Alps may tempt the gaze,
   Their ice-tops glittering in the sun;

So worldly honors often blaze,
  Yet cheerless prove, perhaps, when won.

Then with my sickle in my hand,
  No more a gleaner let me be;
But working with that steadfast band,
  Strike for the fall of Slavery.

  1848.

THE LITTLE BIG MAN.

YOUR Little Big Man is a mighty small thing,
   He puffs, and he swells most importantly round,
Like a brisk cock-turkey he shivers his wing,
   And struts about proudly on his ten feet of ground.

By his dress and his mien you might think him a lord,
   At least he would like you to deem himself so,
Yet never at home, and rarely abroad,
   But others see through his vain-glorious show.

True greatness and worth are seldom mistook,
   For there's something in these which all can perceive;
'T is not in fine cloth, or in proud, vaunting look,
   But the true royal stamp which Nature doth give.

The truly great man is modest and kind,
   Knowing well that before the all-seeing eye
His wisdom and learning are paltry and blind,
   Though reckoned by man of importance most high.

'T is better to pass for just what we are ;
   Our merit the world will soon enough see ;
And if not, what boots it to give it much care,
   So the conscience be clear, and the spirit be free ?

1853.

THE THUNDER-STORM.

O THERE is something in the thunder's peal,
  When bursting from their shroud the lightnings
        dart,
That to my mind more than aught else, reveals
The great Jehovah — the Almighty God.
Naught of the earth in her sublimest scenes,
Such clear, such open evidence displays,
Of a great Ruler — one Omnipotent.
The broad expanse of ocean, from whose realms,
Mysterious, dark and fathomless abodes,
Grace, grandeur and infinity are felt,
The mighty cataract, with thundering voice
Deafening the ear, — the towering mountain's peak, —
Unfold to view, and in a language strong,
Speak of the Almighty Hand that formed them all ;
But faint indeed ! to the tremendous voice,
At which the trembling earth is called to hear,
When, from His great pavilion in the skies,
He causes such terrific fires to glow.
O ! it doth seem, with each repeated shock,
As though His sovereign presence was revealed
Within the open veil — there riding safe
Upon his radiant car, careering through the skies.

A WISH.

TAKE me where Nature spreads around
    Her ample store of woods and fields,
When in the vale of years I 'm found,
    Ere the last hope of pleasure yields.

For so I 've loved the quiet haunts
    Where Poesy makes her holy shrine,
That death himself could scarcely daunt,
    When mid her scenes, this soul of mine.
      1840.

———

ANOTHER.

O WHEN the last sad hour shall come,
    Which must come unto all,
Within my own beloved home
    May its stern bidding fall.

For who would perish far away,
    Upon some foreign strand,
Where no kind friend shall lingering stay,
    To take his farewell hand?

    G

FAREWELL TO WOODLEE.

FAREWELL to thee, Woodlee! thou home of my
      heart,
  With pain I must bid thee adieu;
From all thy fond cherished delights I must part,
  Nor hope them again to renew,—

From thy woods, where so oft alone I have strayed,
  And so oft with those to me dear,
From each sunny nook and deep shaded glade,
  So potent my sad heart to cheer.

Farewell! gentle birds, no longer your song
  Shall welcome my listening ear;
No more shall I guard your newly fledged young,
  And keep your fond hearts from all fear.

Farewell to each scene, so endearingly known,
  Each green bank and sweet flowering bed!
No more your fond master in me shall ye own;
  For others your charms must be spread.

Within thy fair walls, O Woodlee, ere long
   Shall the footsteps of strangers resound;
By the warm, glowing hearth where we all loved to throng,
   Will new forms and new faces be found.

Though far from thee, Woodlee, my footsteps may roam,
.   Though in far distant lands I may be,
Yet still shall I deem thee my once chosen home,
   And fondly look back upon thee.

     1848.

BE HONEST, BOYS.

BE honest, boys! no other way
  Can satisfy your souls' desire;
Let error have its sordid sway,
  But simple Truth your path inspire.

Be honest, boys! let others strive
  For ill-got wealth or ill-got fame:
Far from the snares the base contrive,
  Seek only for an honest name.

Heed not the prize of Fashion's mart;
  Its empty claims and worthless toys
Can only lure the weak of heart:
  Remember this — be honest, boys!

Behold the miseries of wealth!
  Behold the miseries of fame!
What will repay the loss of health,
  Or what supply an honest name?

'T is true, that in the world's esteem,
  An honest name 's at discount now;

But rather weak and humble seem,
    Than at its heartless idol bow.

Let politicians madly rave,
    And sell themselves for guilty spoil;
Let Mammon's subjects dig and save,
    And for their baubles ceaseless toil.

Be honest, boys! no other way
    Can satisfy your soul's desire;
Let worldlings have their short-lived day,
    But Truth alone your path inspire.

1851.

SINCERITY.

I LOVE to see a mind sincere,
    Honest, and earnest for the right,
That naught can tempt, or make to fear,
    Reposing calmly in its might.

I would no common homage pay
    To such a one, whoe'er he be;
Though clothed in rags, despised of men,
    I gladly own his sovereignty:

For such a man to me portrays
    The mark upon his soul divine;
Upon his daily words and ways
    The sun of righteousness will shine.

Such men the world may rarely own, —
    A prouder idol suits their taste, —
But when the mist away has flown,
    Their vineyard seems a dreary waste.

With curious eye in early youth,
    I sought, amid the ranks of men,
The noble bearers of the Truth —
    How few, alas! have met my ken!

1852.

WOODLEE LAWN.

THE grass looks green on Woodlee lawn ;
   The bird is singing on the tree ;
Why should my heart, then, only mourn?
   Why sadness rest alone on me?

He who with sympathetic mind
   So lately viewed these scenes with me,
From each loved haunt now far away,
   Is borne across the stormy sea.

The fields, the woods, though bright and fair,
   Rejoicing in the morning light,
In vain for me their charms prepare ;
   Nor wood, nor field, seem fair or bright.

The grass looks green on Woodlee lawn ;
   The bird is singing on the tree ;
My heart must still be left to mourn,
   'Till he shall safe return to me.

    1852.

MY LITTLE NUN.

MY little Nun, in veil so black,
  That tear dry up, that sigh call back,
Revert less oft to memory's page,
And let kind friends thy grief assuage: —
But hold! I would not stay that tear;
That sigh I would not from thee bear,
For Nature seeks relief to find,
Though friends may prove both true and kind.
Then let the gentle tear-drop fall,
Nor back the escaping sorrow call;
Time shall restore the accustomed track,
My little Nun, in veil so black.

1852.

THE RAIN.

POUR down, O rain! pour down! the thirsty earth
    Gapes her wide mouth from out her countless
      pores
To drink thee in; the trees, refreshed by thee,
Look thankful, and put on a fresher face;
The meadows and the cornfields, scorched so long,
Resume their green and cheerful looks again.
Pour down, O Rain! pour down! a welcome sound,
While pattering on the roof, and 'gainst the panes
Of the small windows in my snug retreat,
Where lone and lonely oft I pass the hours,
Sometimes in pleasant study, — or the pen
Beguiles my solitude; but oftener still
In meditation, when at times my thoughts,
Far in the past, bring forth endeared scenes.
The past! How solemn is the past to all!
Mellowed by distance, all its rougher face
Rubbed down, and polished by the hand of time.
Pour down, O rain! discharge, ye billowy clouds;
Once more fill up the panting brooks and springs.
It comes! the bounteous Hand who holds the fountains

Poureth forth, and in no stinted measure,
In kind remembrance both of man and beast.
O, how dependent man upon his God!
Poor, helpless man! and yet so vain withal!
'T would seem that he who meditates at all,
Or looks beyond the pleasures of the hour,
Must be impressed so strongly of his doom,
That ne'er again the baser walks of life
Could lure him from a just and righteous course.
The blessed rain hath fallen, and the earth
Hath quickly drank it up, and now the trees,
Through every root and fibre, quench their thirst,
And every blade of grass receives its meed.
A happy scene of thanks ascends to Him
Who gave it, witnessed in the freshened face
Of Nature, and the woodland choir's sweet chant.

1855.

SIR WALTER AND LADY SCOTT.

AFTER READING LOCKHART'S LIFE OF SCOTT.

JOINED again in life eternal,
   They who loved so long and well,
Where the year is ever vernal,
Where new buds and blossoms swell,
Hand in hand, mid scenes of beauty,
They securely move along,
Finished all terrestrial duty,
Household cares and gentle song.
Welcomes from the spheres now greet them,
Long lost friends press on to meet them;
Scenes more wondrous than romance
Meet the noble " wizard's " glance;
Prize unknown in page of story,
Deck them in the " crown of glory."

1855.

THE DAY OF REST.

WELCOME to all art thou, sweet day of rest,
　　To rich and poor, forsooth, supremely blest ;
But mostly to the poor and faint of heart,
Who with life's burden feel the bitter smart.
The weary beasts, by kindly hands controlled,
Browse the sweet grass or feed within the fold ;
The din of commerce jars not with its peals,
And manufacture stops her countless wheels.
Not that the day more holy should be deemed,
Or a mere harmless act be wrong esteemed ;
But as a day of ease and sweet content,
Where all that's virtuous may pursue its bent.
All days are holy to the reverent mind,
But this, for rest and peace, is greatly kind.
Then hallowed let it be forevermore,
Stripped of the terrors that enslaved of yore.

AUTUMN TWILIGHT.

CHILL the Autumn wind is blowing;
    Evening throws her veil around;
Soon on hill-top and in valley
    Naught but darkness will be found.

Reft of all the Summer glory,
    Stand the stately forest trees;
Where so late sweet notes re-echoed,
    Swells alone the sighing breeze.

But there is a charm in Autumn
    For the contemplative mind;
Nature aye will teach the reason,
    Truth in all her walks to find.

Leave the school of worldly wisdom,
    Thou of thought and care-worn brow;
And for Him who rules the seasons,
    Learn in solemn awe to bow.

Look abroad upon the landscape,
    Meadows, hills and woods around;

Are not these more grateful teachers
　　Than in human lore are found?

Search the broad, blue, arching heavens
　　To their vast empyrean height;
Think of Him above who made them
　　By His awful word of might.

One clear beam from Nature's teaching,
　　Once received into thy heart,
Shall awaken more true wisdom
　　Than a score from halls of Art.

THE GENTLE VOICE AND QUIET EYE.

NO voice within the vernal grove,
  Not e'en the blue-bird's mellow swell,
Nor meadow-lark or cooing dove,
  Can woman's gentle voice excel.

The softest tones of trembling lute,
  Touched by the hand of magic skill,
The flageolet and warbling flute
  Possess less charm the ear to fill.

The music of the purling rills
  Meandering by the waving trees,
Where violets and daffodils
  Nod gently to the passing breeze:

Though these may cheer the fleeting hour,
  And cause the poet to rejoice,
Yet they unfold not half the power
  Of gentle woman's gentle voice.

The twinkling eye, the sharp, shrill tone
  That pierce the heart as with a knife,

Are fearful e'en amid the crowd,
  But oh! how dreadful in a wife!

The sacred name of Mother ne'er
  Was meant to fall on such a one;
Beside the cradle or the bier,
  I would the harpy ever shun.

How soothing in the hour of grief;
  How thrilling in the hour of joy;
How potent all with sweet relief,
  The gentle voice and quiet eye!

Among the charms that grace the fair,
  Had I before me as my choice,
I'd take, above them all to share,
  The quiet eye and gentle voice.

SPRING'S WELCOME.

THE rich luxuriance of the vernal year
    Is spread on all around; how grand the show!
How sweet the voices of the feathered choir
From yonder thicket, hid among the leaves,
Or flitting o'er the gem-besprinkled meads!
Noisiest of all, the bobolink pours forth
His joyous medley, full of life and cheer,
Flying across the meadows fresh and green;
The golden-robin whistles from the elm,
Where soon shall hang his slender pensile nest;
The gentle quail is piping his clear notes,
Calling "Bob White" to come and join his song,
Or softer warbling for his scattered mates,
Rudely disturbed, perhaps, by my approach;
Anon the cat-bird blusters out his song,
A curious jangle, still endeared to all
Who love wild Nature and her homelier scenes.
But hark! the thrush has mounted yonder elm,
And from its topmost bough is pouring forth
His rich and gushing melody, cheering
All Nature and the soul of man.

O exultation from the love of God!
O Power Divine, expressed in numbers sweet!
Now through yon pasture where the bushes grow,
Let me pursue my meditative way
Unto the woodland, where the spreading oaks
And fresh young maples, the umbrageous pines,
Birches and hemlocks, make a welcome shade.
Here again my feathered friends salute me:
First the ground-robin, scratching 'mong the leaves,
Then quickly mounting on some neighboring bough,
Calling, " Cheweet," or from some loftier perch
Sounding his fuller song of " Pitchodee,"
Or gentler notes expressing, " Please don't grieve."
But soon I hear the wood-thrush' choral song,
Blending so richly with the veery's chant,
That the whole wood becomes a temple vast,
Of rich aerial music, free to all:
And thus are welcomed in the vernal hours.

SECOND SERIES.

1856—1869.

PROEM.

THANK God for poetry.; for what were life
  If all were commonplace and simply prose,
With naught to check the tide of daily strife,
  That in confusion ever ceaseless flows?

How fresh arose upon the morning air
  Those early gushings of old English song,
From bards who drank of sources fresh and fair,
  And loved to mingle Nature's charms among!

The lovely landscape, bright with early dew,
  The lark's loud carol heralding the morn,
Afforded themes forever rich and new,
  Ere pride had taught these simple joys to scorn.

Then through the vale the shepherd's pipe was heard,
  The milkmaid's song, the ploughman's whistle clear,
That mingled sweetly with the song of bird,
  And spake the genius of the vernal year.

The straw-thatched cottage and the moated grange,
  The stately castle and its donjon-keep,
For our home comforts we may well exchange,
  With feudal times, our fields unharmed to reap.

But fields more broad, and skies more deep and fair,
  Are found throughout our own New England's shore,
And we have poets that may well compare
  Among the best old England ever bore.

SOLITUDE.

IN my humble shanty rude,
  Where I pass the graceful hours,
Sweetened by sweet solitude,
  The true spring-time with its flowers,
Many solemn truths I learn
  That are found not in the books,
Ne'er denied to those who yearn
  For them in their chosen nooks ;
For primeval wisdom here
  Finds me ready at her call,
And upon my listening ear
  Oft her kindly whisperings fall,
Telling me in accents clear,
  Known but to the ear within,
That the source of all I hear
  Did with man at first begin :
And in silence as I sit,
  Calmly waiting for the power,

Knowledge to my soul doth flit,
   That in vain I sought before, —
Sempiternal wisdom deep,
   From the endless Source Divine,
Not as creeds and dogmas creep,
   But as doth the day-god shine,
With broad beams of golden light,
   Reaching into every cell,
Driving out the ancient night,
   That my soul in peace may dwell.
Thus I'm taught to look and learn, —
   Rather calmly to receive, —
And from stupid schoolmen turn
   To that which will ne'er deceive ;
To the fountain of all truth,
   To the God of life and love,
Whence the seeking soul, forsooth,
   Learns its happiness to prove.

   1860.

FORTY YEARS AGO.

THE same clear notes the robin sings,
    While on her nest his mate is sitting ;
The oriole, with sable wings
    And golden breast, is by me flitting ;

The martins chatter from the eaves,
    The swallows through the old barn flying ;
The vireos among the leaves
    Of elms in song as erst are vying.

The Summer air is just the same,
    The same blue sky and fleecy cloud ;
A thousand things endeared by name,
    A thousand thoughts my memory crowd.

The harvest-fly, with long-drawn note,
    Salutes the drowsy noontide hour,
And on the soothing breezes float
    The cricket's chimes of mystic power.

The raspberry ripens by the wall
    That bounds the new-mown meadow's side ;

The bayberry and spirea tall
　Are growing still there side by side.

The primrose by the wayside smiles,
　Where soon the golden-rod shall tower ;
Its beauty still my heart beguiles,
　As in my boyhood's sunniest hour.

Midsummer in her glory reigns
　In this our fair New England clime ;
Among her glorious hills and plains,
　How rich this generous flow of time !

In all around I miss no power ;
　I find no change in earth or air —
The same as in life's vernal hour,
　When each new sense was fresh and fair.

No change in Nature's grand domains,
　As rolling on the seasons go ; —
Though man may change, she still remains
　The same as forty years ago.

WINTER EVENING.

THE snow falls on my shanty roof,
    And fiercely drives against the door;
But my warm fire keeps harm aloof,
    And flickers on the hard-pine floor;

Flickers upon the boards and beams
    That form my humble rustic dome,
Where flies enjoy their Winter dreams,
    And wasps and spiders find a home.

Companions of my solitude,
    Ye 're welcome to your chosen nooks,
In this my habitation rude;
    Ye never on my peace intrude,
    But leave me to my thoughts and books.

So let the storm beat loud without,
    If only peace may rule within;
All harping ills I 'll put to rout,
    And deem my solitude no sin.

1858.

H

FALL.

THE maple's changing leaves declare
    The season's hasty close,
Yet still along the wayside fair
    I see the sweet wild-rose;

Still from the orchard's leafy bowers
    The bluebird warbles clear,
And still our garden sports its flowers,
    Though nipping frosts are near.

The Autumn days in youth are sweet,
    For hope then keeps us strong;
But oh! how differently we meet
    When busy memories throng!

1858.

OCTOBER'S CLOSE.

A GOLDEN sunset closed this Autumn day,
   The last sweet day of sweet October's month.
Ye days of golden light, farewell! No more
The woods and fields, my favorite haunts,
Shall smile amid decaying Nature round.
Now welcome darker skies and gusty days,
Keen, cutting winds, and storms of rain and sleet;
Welcome, November! month of wind and storm.
Far down the valley sounds the anthem loud,
Mid rustling leaves that whirl along my path,
Where I again my old companions meet,—
The rabbit and the squirrel, genial friends
That seem to recognize my friendly looks,
And scarcely shun me. Nature now assumes
Her wintry garb; and I once more frequent
These solitary realms sacred to peace.

THE CHICKADEE.

THOU little black-cap, chirping at my door,
    And then saluting, with thy gentle song
Or lonely whistle, my attentive ear,
A hearty welcome would I give to thee,
Thou teacher blest of quietness and peace —
Sweet minister of love for hearts awake
To the rare minstrelsy of field and wood,
Thou constant friend! I hail thee with delight,
Who at this season of rude Winter's reign,
When all the cheerful Summer birds are fled,
Dost still remain to cheer the heart of man!
And though in numbers few thy song is given,
Two tranquil notes alone thy fullest song,
Yet scarcely when the joyous year brings back
The swelling choir of various notes once more,
Have I found deeper or more welcome strains :
For when all nature glows with life again,
When hills and dales put on their vernal gear,
When gentle wild-flowers burst upon our gaze,
With all the exultation of the year,
Our souls, unequal to the heavenly boon,

Are often overwhelmed; and in the attempt
To enjoy it all, drop listless and confused.
But at the close of these sweet sights and sounds,
This grand display of God's enriching power,
The trees all bare, and nature's russet stole
Thrown o'er the landscape, chill must be the heart,
Ingrate to Him who rules the perfect year,
That is not gladdened by thy gentle song.

1859.

THE OLD FOUNTAIN.

HOW rich the well-springs of old English verse,
   Sparkling with dew and freshness ever,
Where poets dream of love, and joys rehearse,
   From whose sweet songs may I be parted never :

For with them and with thee, dear Nature, I
   Have dwelt so long, and so serenely dwelt,
That nothing deeper 'neath the ambient sky,
   In sweet communion hath my spirit felt ; —

From childhood's dawn to manhood and old age,
   The riches of my life, of hope the spring,
Shining from out the glory-lighted page,
   Illumed by Him who plumes the muse's wing.

And I would bid you, friends, wherever found,
   To come and drink of this perennial stream,
The cheer of life in its dull daily round,
   And catch at times of higher truths a gleam :

For man immortal needs some grander aim
   Than just to pander to the body's wants, —

Some soul inspiring theme to light the flame,
  And lead him onward through fair Nature's haunts.

Search then these ancient sources of the muse,
  So full of morning and the love of song, —
Of gentle flowers, whose freshness will diffuse
  A glow of life its sadder walks among.

TO R. W. E.

DEAR, amiable man, of soul sublime,
    How like a tower thou risest to our eyes,
Or like a stately ship of rich emprise,
Laden with choicest freight from some fair clime,
To scatter blessings in a needful time!
Well hast thou wrought thy way through masses deep
Of rampant evils, or through those that sleep,
Yet when awakened charge thee with their crime.
No lack have we on our New England soil
Of gifted spirits, to their country dear,
Who in their noble spheres unceasing toil;
But in the highest walks thou hast no peer.
A Parker or a Beecher strong may plough
The fallow ground, but thou the seed must sow.

1860.

TO THE SAME:

ON READING HIS LINES "TO THE MUSE."

THOU writest of the muse, thou seek'st to find,—
  Whose footsteps lead thee fleeter than the wind.
Thyself a " Beckoner" and " Escape" most rare,
Through the deep mazes of thy fertile mind,
Dost take us all thy rosy gifts to share,
But still thyself we reach not anywhere ;
For higher yet and farther off thou art,
As we draw near unto the chosen spot,
To find that thou hast ta'en a fresher start,
And where thou beckoned'st, there to gain thee not.
Thou " mutablest Perversity," forsooth !
In writing thus about the errant muse,
Whom thou of subtlest wanderings dost accuse,
Thou hast thyself portrayed in very truth !
Still lead thou on, though we may ne'er attain
The promised land of fair content, and true ;
Enough if we may break the encumbering chain,
And haply catch, at times, a Pisgah view.

1860.

A VERNAL ODE.

TO W. E. C.

THE blue-bird has come, and the violet is blooming,
  The love-tinted wind-flower peeps forth from its
      bed,
The heralds of Spring now thickly are coming, —
  Each day some new treasure before us will spread.
The wild geese aloft are flying by daily,
  As northward they hie to their Summer retreat;
Each thing of new life is shining forth gaily,
  The lover of Nature in friendship to greet.

The farmers already their toils are beginning,
  The herring and shad to our river have come;
This gush of new life, so fresh and so winning,
  Invites the pale student mid fresh scenes to roam.
Then leave, brother bard, your brain-taxing labors,
  The charms of the season once more to enjoy,
While the fair, blooming Spring is so rich in her favors;
  For " all work and no play makes Jack a dull boy."

1857.

SUMMER'S CLOSE.

NO longer chants at early morn
  The thrush his mellow song;
Each thing of life then newly born
  Has flown, or perished long.

The blue-bird and the purple finch,
  That late among the trees
So sweetly warbled forth their notes,
  Borne on the gentle breeze;

The oriole and bobolink,
  That cheered the Summer days,
With all the field and woodland choir,
  No longer tune their lays.

The young birds, clamorous for their food,
  Within the orchard's shade,
Long since have sought the neighboring wood,
  And there new homes have made.

Now perched high on some forest tree,
  The jay shouts forth his call,

And startled coveys whir away
    Among the birches tall.

The sweet, fair flowers, that decked the earth,
    And made my walks so glad,
Have fallen scattered on the ground,
    And left me lone and sad.

The rose, that near my window bloomed,
    All wet with morning dew,
And far around the air perfumed,
    Now withered meets my view.

The fields no longer fresh and green,
    The brown and ripened maize,
And birds in flocks together seen,
    Proclaim of shorter days.

So pass away the days of life,
    The Springtime and its flowers,
While mellow Autumn binds the sheaf
    For Winter's lengthened hours.

    1855.

A WORD OF CHEER.

HERE'S a hand to struggling merit,
  And a heart warm with it too;
Ye who hope, but want inherit,
  Let a brother welcome you.

Sons and daughters, cease not striving;
  Youth and courage must prevail;
Let not doubt of faith depriving,
  Cause your noble gifts to fail.

Dearly bought, that glorious treasure,
  For which souls like yours aspire;
Found not mid the haunts of pleasure,
  The reward that you desire:

But through paths of pain and labor,
  Through long years of ceaseless toil,
Comes at length the long-sought favor,
  Harvest rich of genial soil.

God and Nature ever kindly
  Smile upon your grand career;

Heed not, then, if base and blindly
  Pride may at your efforts jeer.

'T is the fate of all true merit
  Long to suffer and to strive,
But keep up your noble spirit,
  And the deeds you do shall live, —

Live when wealth and titles vanish,
  Live and flourish like the tree,
Whose broad arms adorn the landscape,
  Whose strong roots from rot are free.

Not from out the halls of grandeur,
  Not from ranks of worldly fame,
Not where gold and silver glitter,
  Spring the great and good of name.

'Neath some lowly roof we find them,
  Whom no earthly bribe could lure,
Pressed by toil's unyielding mandate,
  Sons and daughters of the poor.

Wealth, with all the pride of station,
  But beclouds the brilliant mind;
They who most adorn their nation,
  From the humbler walks we find.

Lowly lot and brave encounter,
  Doing well your chosen part,
Wise contentment, generous nature,
  Well become the strong of heart.

How much nobler, how much better,
  Honest industry like yours,
Than the wasted hours of pleasure,
  Basely spent mid fashion's lures!

Knowledge gained in such brave struggles,
  Wisdom surely gives the heart;
With these, Nature's noble children,
  Gladly would I take my part.

   1857.

OLD CHARLEY.

ON thy honest face, old Charley,
    Time has set his iron seal;
And thy stiffened limbs, old Charley,
    Age and servitude reveal.

Thou hast been a faithful servant,
    Ready ever at my call;
Strength and courage for my service
    Kindly hast thou given all.

Oft mid pleasant scenes, old Charley,
    Far away from town and noise,
Hast thou borne me through the by-ways,
    Where sweet Nature doth rejoice, —

Happy seeming, as before thee
    Leisurely I walked along,
With thy ears directed forward,
    And thy step so true and strong.

Now though age and weakness check thee,
    The good will doth still remain,

And as erst thou lov'st to take me
   To our favorite haunts again.

In the past, old honest Charley,
   In the past so fairly seen,
Filled with memory's sacred treasures,
   Much, old Charley, thou hast been.

Now in pastures green I turn thee,
   There to graze and take thy ease,
Or beneath the shady maples
   Catch the fresh and cooling breeze.

   1856.

A SUNSET REVERY.

'TWAS Winter, and the close of day,
   Some ten long years, or more, ago,
When by the fire-light's flickering ray,
   I yielded to my musing's flow.

From out my western window far,
   I looked beyond the brown old wood,
And saw the beauteous evening star,
   So glorious in its solitude.

A something richer far than thought,
   O'er my hushed spirit ere long came ;
A something I had never sought, —
   A halo with a living flame.

And so I took my idle pen,
   The sunset hour my ready theme ;
I felt it to be sacred then,
   Though now perhaps a waking dream.

     When the sun has sunk to rest,
     And the gentle twilight falls,

In the chambers of the west,
In those distant pearly halls,
Glimpses of a better land
I imagine I can see,
Where resides that glorious band,
Glorious for eternity.
O ! how infinite the space
Unto my short vision seems,
Speaking of a resting place
For the blessed of our race,
Where eternal daylight beams.
Calmly, reverently I gaze,
As it were, on things divine,
For within that pearly maze
Angel forms and faces shine ;
And amid that radiant band,
Smiling with a heavenly love,
Beckoning with her lily hand,
I behold my long-lost dove ;
That sweet face again I see,
Earnestly regarding me,
Wreathed in beauty as of yore,
Sweeter even than before —
Beaming immortality !
Gracefully her golden hair

Falls upon her shoulders white ;
Seen in that resplendent light,
O, how exquisitely fair !
Silent, anxiously I gaze,
Straining my poor sight to see,
Fearful lest some earthly haze
Come between my love and me :
But the curtain quickly falls,
And I find myself alone ;
Life with duty sternly calls, —
Lo ! my dove again has flown.

1857.

THE SAXON HEART.

THE Saxon heart bears not control;
  Like a strong river on its course,
The tide swells on within the soul,
  O'erpowering every adverse force : —

The brave, good heart, that takes its stand,
  Resisting wrong, defying shame,
Born like a prince to take command,
  Regardless still of praise or blame, —

The matchless heart of bold emprise,
  The conquering heart, the heart so strong,
The heart of heroes, brave and wise,
  The heart that always rights the wrong.

The race that erst, in forest drear,
  The deadly arrow swiftly sped,
Hath dropt the winged shaft and spear,
  And wields the winged thought instead.

The race that once went bravely forth
  To beard the wild boar in his den,
Now meets the tyrant in his wrath, ·
  And boldly claims the right of men.

As in those Saxon days of old
    The bow-string echoed far and wide,
The words of truth ring out like gold,
    The same old spirit sanctified.

The race whence valiant Luther sprung,
    The modern herald of the cross,
Whose words throughout the world have rung,
    And cleared religion of its dross,

Spake out in honest Fox and Penn,
    Inspired a Wesley's fervent heart,
Moved Sidney for the rights of men,
    And Vane to take the freeman's part, —

The race that on the battle-field
    Opposed the tyranny of kings,
Like Hampden, ready life to yield,
    Believing more in men than things, —

And in our day still battles wrong,
    Believing still in knightly deed,
And finds in Phillips' classic tongue
    A voice the bondman's claim to plead.

1860.

AUTUMN.

NOW the golden-rod and yarrow
   By the wayside richly glow,
While the humbler Summer flowers
   'Neath the sterner sceptre bow.

Where the wind-flower early blossomed,
   By the gentle violet's side,
Indian pink and snowy orchis
   Paint the meadows in their pride.

Silent now the sweet, fair songsters,
   That so charmed the vernal prime,
Or for other lands departed,
   To a more congenial clime:

Yet the blue-bird, sweet and gentle,
   Warbles round his favorite haunt;
First to welcome, last to leave us,
   Soothing ever with his chant.

Now the insect choir is lending
   Everywhere its happy strains;

Solemn, sweet, and yet so dirge-like,
  Quieting our heartfelt pains.

Louder now the winds are blowing,
  Sighing through the forest pines;
Walnuts on the boughs depending;
  Drooping now the clustered vines.

From his perch upon the tree-top,
  Loud the jay pipes forth his notes;
Crows are cawing, black-caps whistling, —
  On the air their concert floats.

On the wind, mid dry leaves blending,
  Now the thistle-down floats by,
And the clouds, like snow-piled mountains,
  Sail athwart the azure sky.

Sad monitions Autumn brings us:
  Weary hours we all must feel;
But kind Nature, ever genial,
  Still our wounded hearts can heal.

    1857.

WORKING AT THE MILL.

WORKING at the mill, poor Bessy!
   Working at the mill;
Though thy strength has long been failing,
   Toiling, striving still!

Struggling for thy bread, poor Bessie,
   Struggling for thy bread;
And thy little helpless sisters
   By thy labor fed.

Toiling at the mill, poor Bessy,
   Toiling at the mill;
While thy gentle heart is breaking,
   Working, toiling still.

Hark! the bell is ringing, Bessy;
   Kiss them quick and go;
Leave them to their lonely pastime,
   Haste through rain and snow.

Wasted form and face, poor Bessy,
   Mark thy cruel fate,

Slaving at the loom, poor Bessy,
    From the dawn till late.

Home and friends thou hadst once, Bessy,
    Parents kind and dear,
In old Erin's far-off country, —
    Nothing then to fear.

Working, though thy limbs be failing,
    Working at the mill,
And thy once fair form be ailing,
    Working, striving still.

But good angels watch thee, Bessy;
    Thou art not alone,
For thou hast a home, provided
    At the Father's throne.

Soon thy God will take thee, Bessy,
    And thy tender care,
Where, instead of tattered garments,
    Shining robes ye'll wear.

1857.

THE RIVEN OAK—JOHN BROWN.

FIRM the oak upon the hill-top,
  Though its branches may be torn,
Standeth in its solemn glory,
  Standeth solemn and forlorn.

Though the lightning rend asunder
  And prostrate the noble bole,
Acorns that have fallen under
  Shall increase a thousand fold.

So old Brown of Osawatomie,
  With his sons in blood and death,
Like the dragon's teeth when planted,
  Serried armies shall bequeath.

Nov. 22, 1859.

THE PETITION—JOHN BROWN.

TO H. A. W.

STILL the warm current flows along his veins, —
  His noble heart still beats to freedom true,
And finds a deep response where virtue reigns, —
  His soul sublime, and calm as heaven's own blue.

O thou who hold'st his life-blood in thy hands,
  List to the voice of God that speaks within ;
His life or death depends on thy commands, —
  O, nobly spare him, and escape the sin :

For surely as he dies, upon thy soul
  His blood will leave an everlasting stain.
Spare but thy hand to do a deed so foul,
  For God to thee hath made thy duty plain.
O, spare the brave old man, and thousands here
Will bless thy name, thy future days will cheer.

Nov., 1859.

DAWN—JOHN BROWN.

IN MEMORIAM.

YOU 'VE surely reckoned now without your host,
  O Henry Wise ;
A voice already sounds along our coast,
  Borne from the skies,
That a new saint hath entered heaven's courts,
 Whose open gates receive the welcome guest,
And where the sweetest music ever floats,
 No more by tyrants pierced, he finds his rest,
  His duty all fulfilled.
Peace his reward ; but ah ! no peace for thee,
Proud, cruel land, stained with this infamy,
  Thou who his blood hast spilled.

Sing praises for him, then, the good, the brave —
  Toll on, sad bells ;
Your solemn music, over land and wave,
  The requiem swells
Of one as true as steel, whose noble heart
 Beat with fierce courage in the bondman's cause,

Who with God's poor so greatly chose his part,
And died the victim of accursed laws :
His spirit liveth still !
And lives to haunt the tyrants of mankind,
To wake new zeal in every noble mind,
And nerve heroic will.

Benighted South ! why will ye not awake?
It is already dawn !
From off your eyes the scales of blindness shake ;
No longer scorn
The honest counsel of your truest friends, —
Not they who smile so basely on your sin,
Who have at heart naught but their selfish ends,
And meanly lick the dust, your grace to win !
Not these indeed !
But they who of your danger give alarm,
Who seek your good alone, and not your harm, —
Their counsel heed.

No longer plain John Brown,
But now enshrined a saint,
Such as of olden time
The masters loved to paint.

Dec. 18, 1859.

THE FATAL FRIDAY.*

AGAIN our hearts are destined to be torn ;
   Humanity again is set at naught ;
All our appeals the tyrant treats with scorn,
   And we behold our land with misery fraught.

Men of the North, the tocsin that of yore
   Aroused your fathers to defend their rights,
Sounds the same larum louder than before —
   To boldly meet our foemen in their might.

No longer rest upon your hopes supine —
   Forbearance further will destruction prove ;
Stand for your rights, the oppressors' bounds define,
   And from our shores the curse of slavery move.

     March 16, 1860.

*John Brown, executed Friday, Dec. 2, 1859; Cook, Coppick, Copeland and Green, Friday, Dec. 16, 1859; Stevens and Hazlett, Friday, March 16, 1860; — martyrs for the slave.

TO THE PRESIDENT.

UNTO the danger of the time awake!
   Take heed from him who lost his host of old,
Lest o'er our land some judgment too shall shake
   Our nation's fabric from its tottering hold.

Speak but the word the Lord to thee hath given —
   " Release my people from their bondage sore,"
Ere shall go forth from out the Throne of heaven
   The appalling mandate that was heard of yore.

How long shall we in anxious hope remain?
   Alas! our fear already drowns our hope:
Undo the heavy burdens and the chain,
   And from the weary slave remove the yoke.

Spare, too, more blood, more sacrifice of life:
   Our land already heaves with sighs and groans:
Thy word alone can end the bloody strife:
   Heed thou the orphan's and the widow's moans!

June 18, 1862.

MARGARET FULLER OSSOLI.

THY star, O noble woman, hath not set,
   Though thou in person art no longer here,
But shines more brightly from the clear expanse,
   Our fainting hearts and lingering hopes to cheer.

A cynosure of hope thy life hath proved,
   To thousands who thy presence never saw,
Thou noble champion of the highest truth,
   Thou brave expounder of the heavenly law.

In learning's maze thou trodd'st serenely good,
   For liberty and virtue lent thy life,
Plucked from the hand of fate the ruthless wand,
   And taught our race to love where erst was strife.

Thy country owes thee much, but thy reward
   In higher realms already hath been found,
And generations yet unborn shall learn
   A truer mission from thy noble ground.

How many now, just entering at the porch
   Of life's great temple, take thy outstretched hand,

12

And led by thee a fairer field behold, —
  By thee have learnt in firmer faith to stand!

When death approached amid the whelming waves,
  How calm and true thou mett'st thy ruthless fate,
Bowed to his sceptre, and, resigning all,
  Sank but to rise into a brighter state.

As was thy life, so was thy end portrayed
  By noble virtue and exalted truth,
And when most needed, thou as wont didst find
  The same great spirit that sustained thy youth.

O, what a loss to us who still remain,
  Thou who so well our wayward steps couldst guide!
The wand thou dropt'st now others may assume,
  And we but feebly in thy faith abide.

  1857.

THE LOST MATE.

AN OCTOBER LAY.

GATHERING apples in the orchard,
  On a bright October day —
Sweet the blue-bird warbling near me,
  As when blossoms decked the May;
Suddenly broke peals of laughter,
  From two happy hearts, I ween,
One of them my own fair daughter,
  And the other beauty's queen.

Bounding, shouting, they came towards me,
  Drowning soon the blue-bird's song,
But instead, a music sweeter
  From their voices swept along,
Full of life and full of pleasure;
  My worn heart rejoiced to see
Youth and beauty in such measure,
  Crowned with love and social glee.

One short year alone has vanished,
  Since the record of that day,

And again the fruit has ripened —
    Soft the blue-bird chants his lay ;
In the orchard once more gathering
    From the trees their golden store,
But in memory's mingled treasure
    I behold the barren ore, —

For no laughter ringing greets me —
    Naught to glad my pensive heart,
And alone my child now meets me,
    From her loved mate torn apart ;
That rich voice is hushed forever —
    Closed for aye those lovely eyes,
And beneath the flower-strewn hillock,
    Her dear form in silence lies.

Hallowed be the dear old orchard,
    Each fair tree with interest spread,
For the past, so sad and sacred,
    And the brave young spirit, fled.
Sacred every spot and record,
    Where our lost loved ones have been,
Monitors to teach us wisdom,
    Ere shall fade earth's latest green.

1857.

THE FALLOW FIELDS.

I LOVE these brown old fallow fields,
   Where so much peace and beauty reign;
Their solitude more treasure yields
   For me, than fields of waving grain.

These old stone walls, with mosses clad,
   In broken ranges spread around,
Frame their own tale, so true and sad,
   And well adorn such hallowed ground.

The golden-rod and yarrow white,
   The velvet mullein's yellow flower,
Afford an ever welcome sight,
   And gladden Summer's latest hour.

Once these old fields, now worthless deemed,
   And left alone, all stripped and bare,
With glistening maize in glory teemed,
   And well repaid the farmer's care.

That brave old race that fought the woods,
   Who fenced, and ploughed, and tilled the soil,

Lie hushed in Nature's solitudes,
  And Nature claims their fields of toil.

Yon old gray farm-house, drear and lone,
  Whose blackened roof must ere long fall,
With childhood's merry voices rang,
  And rang with busy housewife's call.

The blue-bird comes as he was wont,
  And builds within the hollow tree;
The robin chants his vernal song,
  Though none regard his minstrelsy.

Where once the garden, in its pride,
  With homely crops and flowers smiled,
Where gleesome children loved to hide,
  · Now spring the dock and sorrel wild.

As wont the brook glides on its way,
  The alders still its banks adorn,
The trout still snaps his winged prey,
  And black-birds hail the rising morn.

The seasons roll on as before,
  Summer and Winter, Spring and Fall,
The same blue skies as seen of yore,
  The same dark, threatening thunder pall.

The full-orbed moon looks blandly down
  On these old fields, and farm-house gray ;
The same sweet smile, the same dark frown,
  Still keep their old accustomed way.

So Nature, ever fresh and strong,
  Though men may fail and pass away,
Rejoicing in her pastoral song,
  Maintains her calm supremacy.

    1857.

TO W. C. B.

—

"O thou great movement of the Universe,
Or change, or flight of time, for ye are one,
That bearest silently this visible scene
Into night's shadow, and the streaming rays
Of starlight, whither art thou bearing me?
I feel the mighty current sweeping on,
Yet know not whither."

AN EVENING REVERY.

—

DEAR poet! in thy graphic lines I see
    The strong man wrestling with life's iron doom,
Striving in hope to obtain the mastery,
    And from death's portals to dispel the gloom.

With no rebellious heart I too have sought
    To find a solace for my anxious soul,
And with conflicting doubts and fears have fought,
    That peace might exercise her sweet control.

I sympathize with thee, dear bard of truth!
    With trembling faith I seize thy outstretched hand,
For I have left behind the days of youth,
    And gather glimpses of the distant land.

Though dim the light that bounds my lessening way,
  With rankling thorns and nettles oft bestrewn,
In the faint hope that soon may break the day,
  I strain my eyes to keep it still my own.

Proud teachers of the word ye name of God,
  Who so familiarly his plans explain,
How little know ye of that dread abode
  Ye paint for mortals, made for joy or pain!

With humble mien the seeking heart explores
  The haunts of nature, haply there to find,
Among the riches of her genial stores,
  The long-sought treasure for the yearning mind, —

Cons with fresh zeal the scrolls of wisdom o'er,
  To find the key to life's mysterious page, —
But leaves unreaped the fields of classic lore,
  Whose glowing charms our early years engage.

Therefore, dear bard! and ye, companions dear,
  Whose waning years forewarn of no return,
Receive a brother's sympathetic tear,
  A brother's hand unto that gleaming bourne.

  1857.

THE IMPROVISED DANCE.

LIKE the Indian dance of old,
  Far within the forest shade,
Showing forth the spirit bold,
  That no foeman e'er dismayed,—

Like the dancing of the Hours,
  Tripping on with merry feet,
Triumphing o'er earthly powers,
  Yet with footsteps all must greet, —

Like the Fauns and Satyrs too,
  Nimbly leaping in the grove,
Now unseen, and then in view,
  As amid the trees they move, —

Like the leaves by whirlwind tossed,
  In some forest's valley wide,
Scattered by the Autumn frost,
  Whirling madly side by side, —

Thus, and still mysterious more,
  Our philosopher did prance,
Skipping on our parlor floor
  In his wild improvised dance.
1857.

WALDEN.

HERE once a poet most serenely lived,
  A poet and philosopher, forsooth,
For in him both have joined, and greatly thrived,
  And found content before the God of Truth ; —

A plain-set man, a man of culture rare,
  Who left an honor on old Harvard's walls ;
An honest man, in search of Nature's fare ;
  The spot more rich where'er his shadow falls.

Near by the shore his cabin reared its head ;
  With his own hands he built the simple dome ;
And here, alone, to thought and study wed,
  He found a genial, though a humble home.

From the scant produce of a neighboring field,
  Tilled by his hands, he got his honest bread ;
But Nature for him greater crops did yield,
  In rich abundance daily for him spread.

The woods, the fields, the lake, and all around,
  Both man and beast, and bird, and insect small,

In his keen mind a shrewd expression found —
    For truth and beauty he discerned in all.

A jurist learned in Nature's court supreme,
    A wise physician, priest, and teacher too,
For whom each sphere reveals a ready theme,
    And wisdom is exhaled, both old and new.

While others unto foreign lands have gone,
    And in old footsteps travelled far and wide,
This man at home a richer prize hath won,
    From fresher fields, unknown to wealth and pride.

His own good limbs have borne him well about,
    Whose constant use hath made him staunch and strong,
As many a luckless wight hath proven out;
    And Concord soil in him hath found a tongue.

Henceforth her hills, her gently flowing stream,
    Her woods and fields, shall classic ground become,
And e'en the village street with interest beam,
    Where one so nobly true hath found a home.

To Walden pond the ingenuous youth shall hie,
    And mark the spot where stood the hermitage;

But ye who seek mid glittering scenes to vie,
   Let other haunts your vanity engage.

Go on, brave man ! in thy own chosen way —
   How many ills of life thou dost escape !
Thy brave example others shall essay,
   And from thy lessons happier lives may shape —

Shall learn from thee to find a ready store
   Of choicest treasures spread before their eyes ;
For Nature ever keeps an open door,
   And bids a welcome to the good and wise.

   1860.

A WINTER SONG.

O'ER fair New England's hills and plains,
    Old Winter drives his rugged car;
No monarch more sublimely reigns;
    No serfs than his more loyal are.

Throned on his mountains, Green and White,
    He calls his vassals to his hand;
The storm-gods, wrestling in their might,
    Rush swiftly forth at his command:

Old Boreas, leader of the hosts
    Of rain and snow, from Newfoundland,
And Caurus, from the ice-bound coasts
    Of broad Superior's farthest strand: —

Raging and roaring, on they come!
    Each in their ruler's court to vie,
Contending till they meet their doom,
    And in fair Summer's bosom die.

So love shall melt the chains of ire,
    The only Summer of the heart;

So kindness soothe contentions dire,
    And from our wounds extract the smart.

No stinted monarch is our King!
    His iron will brooks no control;
His minstrels of his valor sing;
    His messengers require no goal;

Where'er he bids them, forth they go;
    The wild-geese are his heralds bold;
The mountain streams that rushing flow,
    By his command their torrents hold.

The great white clouds, that restless poise
    Amid the depths of upper air,
Discharge their burdens at his voice,
    And clothe the hills, and moorlands bare.

The lakes where Summer loved to dwell,
    Where gentle breezes loved to blow,
Roused from their sleep, in billows swell,
    Or sleep again in ice and snow.

The forests roar as they are wont;
    The cataracts growl mid rocks and ice;

Old ocean rears his foaming front,
  And storms the beach in thundering voice.

Scattered around the rocky shore,
  Lie fragments of the stranded bark,
While all unharmed the sea-gulls soar,
  Or swoop into the caverns dark.

By frozen streams the red-deer roves,
  Or seeks a shelter from the storm
Among the pine and hemlock groves,
  That smiling shield his graceful form.

Within his mountain home, the bear
  In some dark cave securely sleeps,
While through the thicket springs the hare,
  Or rabbit from his covert peeps.

The fox steals forth at close of day,
  To snatch the partridge from his perch,
Or from the farm-yard seeks his prey:
  No place too sacred for his search.

Upon the sunny, sloping hills,
  Are homes and hearts most true and brave,

Where through old Winter's threatening chills,
  The glowing hearth from harm shall save.

Who loves not the New England home, —
  The modest farm-house, low and gray,
Whence health and beauty sweetly come,
  To drive the gloom of life away?

In rural scenes contentment thrives,
  And plenty crowns the rustic board ;
Though Winter round his dwelling drives,
  The farmer sits, our truest lord.

Then rule, old monarch of our land !
  For we thy loyal subjects are :
We cheerly bow at thy command,
  Thy blessings and thy chidings share.

    Feb., 1862.

      J

THE KING OF TARKILN HILL.

I CALL him "king of Tarkiln Hill,"
  Though but a sturdy yeoman he ;
For whoso well the soil doth till,
  Possesseth truest majesty.

His home is on the breezy height
  That overlooks Acushnet's vale,
Illumined by the dawn's first light,
  And cooled by Summer's passing gale.

Beneath his axe the old woods fell,
  The stones he piled in fences round,
And now his barns with plenty swell,
  His cattle graze the fertile ground.

His woodlands yield him still a store
  Of fuel for the neighboring town,
His pockets craving little more, —
  Oft you will see him going down.

No monarch seated on his throne,
  Beneath a gilded canopy,

Can boast a grandeur more his own,
   Than with his cart and dobbin, he.

Advancing years now claim release
   From labor's most fatiguing toil,
And so he often takes his ease,
   While others till his yielding soil.

His honest liege-man, " Uncle Sam,"
   Is constant, daily, at his post, —
In youth a lion, now a lamb,
   And still by some esteemed a host.

Give " Uncle Sam " his daily prog,
   And eke his dear tobacco-weed,
And he will at his labor jog,
   Break up the ground and sow the seed.

Of girls and boys, a giant race,
   Our king hath scattered through the land,
And may he long be spared to grace
   Old Tarkiln Hill, and keep command.

I call him " king of Tarkiln Hill,"
   For who can better claim the name

Than one whose ready hand and will
Have wrought the title to his fame?

So let us sing, "Long live the king,"
And heavenly treasures daily hoard,
While time goes on with noiseless wing,
And peace and plenty crown his board.

1862.

IN MEMORIAM.

—

TO H. D. T.

—

O HENRY! in thy new-born sphere of life,
  Thy present home, though hidden from our view,
Does not thy spirit linger still around
Thy much loved Concord? visit'st not thou still
Thy favorite haunts, by river, hill, and dale,
Through lonely woods, or over barren plains,
Where once the ploughshare passed long years ago,
And where with thee I once so gladly roamed,
Through Winter's snow, or Summer's fervent heat,
To " Baker farm," or to the beetling Cliff
That overlooks the gentle river's course,
Or to thy Walden, " blue-eyed Walden " called
By that much gifted man, thy chosen friend,
Companion of thy walks and rural life?
With thee I've sat beside the glowing hearth
Of one so grand in thought, so pure of aim !
New England's keenest, wisest scrutineer,
A poet, too, endowed with rarest gifts,
And listened to the converse thou and he,

So like, and yet so unlike, often held.
Intelligent and wise, and deeply learned,
I found ye both ; both scholars, rich and rare ;
But in the book of Nature no peer hadst thou,
Whether in words expressed of glowing thought,
From deep philosophy revealed of old,
Or in the fields or woods, or by the shore
Of the great ocean thou didst love so well,
And where with pilgrim steps thou often went'st.
No plant escaped thy ever-searching eye ;
No bird or beast, however rarely found,
But thou didst find.   Unknown Indian wares,
By thy divining wand, though centuries hid,
Came forth to view, and thou their history told'st.
And 'neath another roof all browned with age,
And overhung by one great sheltering elm,
Where dwells a seer decreed to solemn thought,
Amid old books and treasures rare to see,
And learned of wisdom and devout of heart,
A bishop worthy of the apostolic age,
We sometimes met to pass a thoughtful hour
In sweet discourse on themes of lofty tone.
I see ye, too, in memory's faithful glass,
As last I saw ye, brave and worthy pair !
The white haired sage, with deep and solemn words

Sonorously expressed; thy quick reply,
Thy eyes all glowing with supreme good sense;
A genial pair, though of unequal age.
Thou worthy man! so noble and so brave!
How much I miss thee, friend and teacher too!
Thou gentle man! thou purest of the pure,
And wisest of the wise, best of the good!
How saint-like and sublime thy walk on earth!
Truly, I never shall behold thy like again.
But whensoe'er old Concord's pleasant realms
Rise to my mind, thou as her chiefest son
Will haunt her as the spirit of her groves,
Her moorland fields, and river famed in song,
And marked in history's page by scenes of blood:
For here, as often told, their yeoman sires
Met the proud Briton, and defied his steps, —
Some falling bravely for their country's right.
And now in coming time linked with this tale,
So often told e'en yet to household groups
Of listening youngsters with wide staring eyes,
Thy honored name shall be remembered too,
Remembered by the good and wise long lustrums hence,
As one who in an age of much dismay,
Lived a serene, a pure and holy life.

1863.

THE OLD MILL-DAM.

OUR village cannot boast of many charms, —
  A simple, straggling hamlet, — but the view
From yonder hill-top, through the river's course,
Affords us many fair and rural scenes ;
And at this season, from the vernal flood,
Our ancient mill-dam magnified becomes,
And in its mimic roar grandeur suggests.
Thus, while I sit enjoying the deep sound
That rises from the stones beneath, Fancy
Her pleasing exaggeration lends me,
And the rich waterfalls and cataracts
That greeted once my youthful eyes and ears
Are brought before my mind in living truth.
Again I see thee, thou great parent fall,
Niagara, as once I saw thee years ago,
When swollen e'en beyond thy usual power
By the Spring rains, thou then appeared'st.
Near thirty years agone — alas ! 't is true —
So much of time from me has slipt away.
How rose my soul then at this glorious sight,
Enraptured with its rare sublimity !

Thy falls too, Trenton, rushing down their course,
O'er rocks and ridges most superbly grand
And beautiful, I also then beheld,
Passing a holy Sabbath there alone,
Wandering among the ever changing scenes
For miles along thy dark and dangerous banks,
Mid evergreens and grotto dripping rocks.
And thy far-sounding fall, swift Genesee,
At this fair season eagerly I sought.
For in their peaceful grandeur I could feel
The sense of greatness in God's mighty works,
Unaccompanied with danger, since
For me the mere terrific has no charm,
But deeply agitates my wavering nerves.
In later times, with one to me most dear,
The graceful Montmorenci I beheld,
And not long after, Chaudiere's wild fall,
So picturesque within its woody glen.
But to return to this our ancient dam,
That hath so led me in the retrospect,
I am content to listen to its roar,
And view the pleasant scenes around.
Across the stream, a hill and crowning wood,
Where hie the partridge and the gentler quail,
And woodchuck in the sheltering banks.

J2

The river, winding through the bordering woods,
Flows gracefully, and at yon shady nook,
O'erhung with pines and broad umbrageous oaks,
I love to plunge into the gliding stream,
When Summer's enervating heat prevails,
And feel myself refreshed and cheered again :
How great the blessing they alone can know,
Who cleanliness and rural quiet love, —
To godliness so near allied.
Upon the other bank, so soft and still,
A quaint ancestral farm-house stands alone,
Whose gambrel roof looks back to long past days,
Counting within its walls four generations
Who have come and gone — one only left
Of all who called the humble house their home ;
Old fields, once graced by toiling hands,
Now left to Nature ; old barn and corn-house,
Leaning with decay and with moss o'ergrown ;
Here and there a cow, or rustic laborer,
Dot the scene, and form a picture for my eye,
So calm and soothing, that I often seek
The peaceful spot, and seated there alone,
Dwell on the landscape with a sweet content,
Nor ask for pictures to adorn my walls,
While Nature liberally supplies me,

Ready at hand, such as no art can give,
However cunning be the artist's hand, —
Works of the great Master, glorious in the least,
And perfect in them all.   Here, too, I learn
To raise my soul in adoration, and
Return back to the world with strengthened faith.

1863.

THE MORROW.

THOUGH the wind is blowing fiercely,
  And the snow is falling fast,
Hopes of Spring-time cheer the memory, —
  Storm and tempest soon are past.

Then comes forth the genial sunshine,
  And the earth will smile again ;
Flowers are waiting in the meadows —
  Grass for April's pleasant rain.

So, when sorrow may surround us,
  And the chilling wind may blow,
Let us look beyond the present,
  Whence our blessings ever flow, —

Unto Him, the great, good Giver
  Of all clear or cloudy skies ;
And though present ills afflict us,
  O'er them all our hopes shall rise.

1863.

SPRING IS COMING.

THE Spring, dear friends, is close at hand, —
   I hear the blue-bird in the trees;
  I hear it in the morning breeze,
And voices rising o'er the land.

The sparrow from the old rail-fence
   Proclaims it in his song so clear,
  His song, to childhood ever dear,
Awakening life to every sense.

The black-bird, garrulous and free,
   From out the lowland alders sings,
  Or sails upon his red-capt wings,
Still keeping up his "konkaree."

The woodpecker sends forth his cry,
   A herald true of milder days,
As, perched upon the maple high,
   He lends his voice in general praise.

The wild-geese now are flying o'er;
   From southern climes they onward come

Unerring to their northern home,
Seeking some favorite distant shore.

All things conspire to swell the strain
    That God in goodness doth abound;
    It cometh from the teeming ground,
It singeth through the shooting grain.

    1866.

EMMA.

THOU graceful offering from the god of day,
  The pure, bright morning shining in thy face,
Through thy fair locks reflects the golden ray,
  And in thy eye the pure blue sky we trace.

Dear shrined image of immortal life,
  May peace and hope thy pathway ever bless;
Remote from fashion's vain, inglorious strife,
  Mayst thou e'er walk mid scenes of pleasantness.

Seek in the haunts of Nature's fair domain,
  Where sings the wood-thrush, and the violet blows,
The surest solace for each heartfelt pain,
  The sacred source from which much wisdom flows.

Simplicity with truth is ever wed,
  And they who joy in these great hope shall find;
Though friends prove false and costlier stores be fled,
  A rich resource for them is left behind.

The schools of art are oft beset with pride;
  Too much of dross among their gold is found:

But Nature spreads her lessons far and wide,
    And with rare wisdom all her haunts abound.

Therefore, dear child, the knowledge thou wouldst gain,
    In books alone thou surely ne'er wilt find :
Like sowers of the soil, these drop the grain ;
    The harvest only springs within the mind.

Thy heart keep open to the force of truth,
    Thy mind receptive of her gracious boon ;
She with rich knowledge shall adorn thy youth,
    And with bright lustre cheer life's latest noon.

        1858.

NOONTIME.

FROM UNDER THE SASSAFRAS-TREE.

THE quail is whistling on the wall
  That skirts the wood so fresh and green ;
His mate is listening to his call,
  Beneath the alder's leafy screen ; —

The robin and the tuneful thrush
  Salute me as I pass along,
And every tree and every bush
  Rejoices in the tide of song ; —

While from my labor in the field
  I lay my shining hoe aside,
And as I rest to musing yield,
  Or into gentle slumbers glide.

The season in its richest dress
  Now greets the lover's ardent gaze,
For Nature ever waits to bless
  The hearts that seek her kindly ways.

How soft and calm the heavenly blue,
　　The huge white floating clouds between !
　　Of hope and joy a sign, I ween,
Where scenes of bliss shall greet our view.

With gratitude for favors past,
　　My soul uprises to our God,
And by obedience hopes at last
　　To shun the chastening of His rod.

Why, mid such glories spread around,
　　Should we forget to render praise
To Him whose goodness doth abound,
　　Whose wisdom ever marks his ways?

O that mankind could live in peace,
　　And brother seek his brother's weal !
Lord ! grant that bloodshed soon may cease ;
　　Our Nation's sore affliction heal.

　　　1864.

CHEER.

THE world still holds together strong, my boys!
  And a good God rules over all things here;
The seasons in their glory bring fresh joys,
  And with unyielding faith we've naught to fear.

Be of good cheer, accept the present good,
  Nor borrow ill the morrow may not know;
Take freely of kind Nature's daily food,
  And let your hearts in daily worship bow.

In virtue only can true bliss be found;
  Let us then seek from the eternal Source
The riches that so graciously abound,
  And steadily pursue a righteous course.

1865.

THE LAPSE OF TIME.

IN youth our years pass very slow,
   Our months and weeks seem very long ;
In manhood they 've an even flow,
   And pleasant sounds their fervid song.

But O ! when age and weakness come,
   How swiftly then the cycles fly !
Happy indeed if we a home
   Can in the land of bliss espy !

When in the vale of years I go,
   May He who kindly hears my prayer
A balm supply for every woe,
   And take me to his Sovereign care.

Upon His mighty arm alone,
   In my prostration would I lie ;
A Saviour's blood may e'en atone
   For sins like mine, so deep of dye.

1865.

HAPPY MEDIOCRITY.

I'VE no pretentions to keep up;
  I'm but a common man,
One of the multitude who pass
  Through life on Nature's plan, —

A simple, honest man, I trust;
  Nor do I ask for more;
Let others seek for wealth and rank,
  And heap up store on store.

None do I scorn, I envy none,
  But wishing well to all,
Would hope at last to rest in peace,
  When He who rules shall call.

Most truly do I envy not
  Those who from pride of place
Must keep a constant watch and ward,
  Lest they themselves disgrace, —

Disgrace, such as the world accounts,
  And not as God declares,

In dress or word, or look, perhaps,
  And countless petty cares.

Of simple pleasures, life affords
  To every one a share,
And that which best with peace accords,
  Is scattered everywhere:

For God is good, and by his grace
  We all may learn to know
How little that men most esteem
  Is needed here below.

The rivalry that haunts the crowd,
  Each other to outvie,
The little great, the money proud,
  Bespeak but vanity.

And so e'en in religious things,
  Where pride should never come,
We see Ambition plumes her wings,
  And Mammon finds a home:

For not content with earthly spoil,
  The aspirant for fame

Finds naught too sacred for his moil,
  Too precious for his game.

And thus we in the church behold
  Vain-glory, ease, and pride;
While piety, in humble mold,
  Is rudely thrust aside.

Fear not, then, ye of nobler mind,
  But leave them to their will;
Enough if ye at last may find
  The Lord, your cup to fill.

  1865.

THE RIGHT PLACE.

KEEP in thy place, and be not ever striving
    To reach some point which nature may deny ;
Of many joys thou art thyself depriving,
    That all unheeded in thy pathway lie.

Spurn not to take them, though they may seem humble ;
    Life's harvest is made up of little things ;
Be thou content, nor with thy fortune grumble,
    But ever thankful for the good it brings.

Thou hast a place which thou canst fill with credit,
    If thou but do thy duty day by day ;
It may not be, perhaps, all thou dost merit,
    But God will every sacrifice repay.

How many in the walks of life are striving
    To make appearance unto others' eyes,
Instead of keeping to an honest living,
    And merit thus approval of the wise !

To deck the person, or with vain ambition
    To seek for rank among the rich and great,

But weakness show ; or worse, a base fruition —
 The product only of a fallen state.

Keep this in mind, that goodness is far better
 Than all that human pride may grandeur deem :
The one gives grace, the other but a fetter ;
 One proves true wealth, the other but a dream.

1866.

K

A SEA PICTURE.

A SHIP came thundering down the Baltic sea,
   A huge old-fashioned Swedish man-of-war;
Her broad protruding bows received the brunt
Of the great seas, and threw the spray on high,
Foaming far o'er the bulwarks strong and deep.
Anon upon the crested wave she rode,
As gallantly as lighter crafts are wont,
And then far down, as though she ne'er would rise,
Into the very bowels of the deep
She plunged, but slowly rose on high again;
And so all day, a dark portentous day,
She made short headway, beating to and fro.
At night the lightning shot athwart the sky,
And howling through the rigging rushed the gale;
Sail after sail, and yard and stay were stript,
And when the morning came at last once more,
The huge old vessel seemed a very wreck, —
Men at the pump, and jurymast upraised,
And tattered canvas spread, the old torn flag
Flapping from out its staff; and crippled thus,

She seeks to reach the nearest anchorage
Or seaport town along the stormy coast, —
A scene of pity, yet so picturesque
That well the artist might her form portray.

1866.

THE STRÜGGLE.

ERE long, through fog and mist and doubt,
I hope at last my way to wrestle out;
And much of that by some thought very odd,
Will then be seen to be ordained of God:
For not in hate, but love, I too have striven,
And humbly sought to know the will of heaven;
For man and beast, by cruelty assailed,
My voice and strength have never basely quailed,
But ever kept a heart to keenly feel
For all beneath oppression's iron heel.

GOD'S GOODNESS.

I THINK, my friend, the case is simply here,
    To some our God is love, to others fear:
As in the heart ourselves we truly are,
Is God revealed.   He is both near and far.
To those who love his presence he is near;
To those who hate it he doth far appear.
That God is love, no Christian can deny;
But 't is the good alone can this espy.
If we ourselves are distant, hard, and cold,
The same will God himself to us unfold.
And so it may be with the life to come, —
To some a prison prove, to others home.
The freedom of the will to man is given,
And he himself can make a hell or heaven.

1866.

MY QUEST.

O LORD! I 've sought to find
    Thy church among mankind,
  Thus far in vain!
I often find instead,
A weight like that of lead,
  That gives me pain.

But scattered all around,
Thy goodness I have found,
    And thy disciples, too,
Men who in word and deed
Have found the heavenly seed;
    Alas! howe'er, too few.

Yet still thy church doth stand,
And will in every land,
    Until the earth and sea
Shall know thee and obey,
And through that better way
    Find strength and hope in thee.

    1866.

NEW YORK.

O COMPLICATION of all evil,
　　And complication of all good;
Where thousands worship but the Devil,
And thousands also worship God!
O wretchedness beyond compare!
O filth and rags, and stagnant air!
O glittering wealth and poverty,
And rosy health and misery!
The palace and the hovel vie
To take the palm of victory.
Centre of all that's good and bad,
Of all that's cheerful, all that's sad!
May God in mercy spare the best,
And in his wisdom purge the rest.

1867.

THE NEW YORK DUSTMAN'S BELLS.

OF all comical sounds in heaven or earth,
    A combination of sadness and mirth,
There 's nothing to my imagining tells
More wonderful tales than the dustman's bells,
        As wrangling, jangling, to and fro,
        Their notes are heard wherever you go.

Witches and goblins fill the air;
Oaths and curses mingle with prayer;
From gutter to eaves, and very house-top,
Such queer looking people I fancy may pop, —
        As wrangling, jangling, to and fro,
        Their notes are heard wherever you go.

The ghosts of old Dutchmen long hidden appear,
With their "donder and blitzen," "mine Gott," and
            "mynheer";
And mid the strange bluster, and jostle, and jam,
Our "Gotham" is lost in "New Amsterdam," —
        As wrangling, jangling, to and fro,
        Their notes are heard wherever you go.

For among these old rags and fragments so packed,
From many a garret and cellar ransacked,
Are bits of old garments a century old,
That marvellous bits of old history unfold, —
    As wrangling, jangling, to and fro,
    Their notes are heard wherever you go.

And not unmusical, too, are these bells,
Reminding the ear of pastoral dells,
Of scenes far away in the country so dear,
Where there's nothing from want and wrong to fear, —
    As wrangling, jangling, to and fro,
    Their notes are heard wherever you go.

Ring on! ring on! ye quaint old bells,
And rouse each house with your constant knells;
But rarely, I fancy, shall rhymer like me
Find in your rude notes such weird minstrelsy,
    As wrangling, jangling, to and fro,
    Their notes are heard wherever you go.

    1867.

OLD ENGLAND.

HOME of my fathers long, long years ago,
    I feel for thee a strong and filial love,
And next to my own beloved native land,
Prize thee above the nations of the earth.
I know that thou hast many blots upon
Thy shield, and cruel art at times, whene'er
Thy rule is forced upon its victims;
Through blood I know that thou hast risen high
In glory, by the scale of nations: still,
For the great and good spirits thou hast borne,
I love thee.   Land of Howard, Wilberforce,
And " Nature's darling," the true Christian bard,
The gentle Cowper, dear to every heart
Attuned to truth and virtue's lovely haunts;
And in these later days, and our own time,
The much-loved home of Wordsworth, Coleridge,
And Southey, unto whom I owe so much; —
For these, and many more of ancient time,
As well as modern, do I entertain
For thee, O sea-girt isle, an affection;
And in earlier years, through thy inspired bards,

K2

A strong desire, as yet unrealized,
To visit thy fair realms, and wander o'er
Thy scenes historic, see the homes and haunts
Of those whose works have ever been to me
Friends and companions in the walk of life.
How dear indeed the spot that rendered birth
To ye, dear Sons of Poetry divine,
Scattered all o'er thy soil, Britannia,
And through the Cambrian and the Scotian hills,
And o'er green Erin.   Oft in thought I go
Through gray old abbeys and crumbling castle walls,
Mantled with ivy, beauteous in decay,
And dwell on themes found in historic page ; —
A thousand years ago, when mailed knights
Rode forth on errands to the farthest east,
Or met in tournament with shield and lance.
But scenes of modern time delight me more,
And oft I trace with reverential steps
The haunts of Cowper, portrayed in his Task ;
Visit his garden and his Summer-house,
His walks at Olney by the banks of Ouse,
The woods of Weston, Sir John Throckmorton's grounds,
The " Wilderness," the " Lime Walk," and the " Chase,"
Where stands the Yardley oak, renowned in verse ;
Seen in the distance, Olney's tapering spire,

And Emberton's square tower with chime of bells,
That so much charmed the poet's listening ear;
The " Hall," where Cowper met his " Lady Frog "
And " Catharina," patrons of his muse,
And constant friends until the poet's death, —
These, and the like, would tempt my wandering steps
From scenes of fashion and from prouder sights.
The bard of Avon, too, would claim my love,
And with delighted steps I stray along
The village street to Charlecote's fair woods,
Where story says the poet purloined deer
When in the heyday of his roystering youth,
And was arraigned before the angry Squire;
Thence to the church where rest his honored bones,
Yet undisturbed, as was the poet's wish,
And curse pronounced on the offender's head; —
Forgetting not upon my pilgrimage
The " Leasowes," Shenstone's rural seat,
Drummond of Hawthornden, and banks of Ayr,
Renowned as the ploughman-poet's home,
The land of Burns, endeared to every muse.
Thus would I wander through our Fatherland,
Mid scenes endeared to virtue and to truth,
The homes of godlike genius, that have kept
Their land from sinking 'neath a barbarous sway.

Far greater than her warriors, men of blood,
Her Marlborough, or Wellington, I deem
Her sons of song, such as glorious Milton,
The bard of Olney, and of Rydal Mount,
And Tennyson of our own time, whose verse,
Though often shaded by a sombre muse,
Still rises with the great harmonic chant,
From Chaucer's key-note of old English verse
Down to the present day of choral song.

1866.

IN MEMORIAM.

—

G. G. C.

OBIIT XXV JUNII, MDCCCLXVII.

—

" He must not *rest* upon his *lowly* bier
Without the meed of some melodious tear."

—

THE fatal draught to its last poisonous dregs,
  Sick of the world and tired of life, he drank,
Then laid him down for his unwaking sleep,
And to his God resigned the life He gave.
Unhappy man! but ah! who can thee blame?
Rather, who feels not pity for thy fate —
Pity and kindly sympathy and love
For one himself so gentle, and so kind withal?
Poor C*****, — yet why poorer than ourselves?
For have we aught to boast, are we so strong,
So self-reliant in our righteousness
Or worldly wisdom, that we can afford
To look upon thee as of weaker clay,
Or less Heaven-favored than our feeble selves?
Indeed! not so: we are in truth but poor,

Dependent, faltering, transitory forms,
Pensioners for daily bread, and every good.
Ah! who can tell the suffering, anguish
Of soul and body — fortune, health, all gone,
A burden to himself, and to his friends,
At least in fancy, yet not less severe —
Of him now sleeping in the arms of death,
No more to wake, until the final trump
Shall call the dead from out their narrow homes?
How quiet is his sleep! the busy mart
And all the stir and din of merchandise
Disturb him not — no care distracts his mind,
Closed are the portals of each earthly sense,
His day is o'er, his last sad debt is paid!
O! sad indeed, that in our very midst,
Where Christian men and women daily meet,
And churches stand on almost every street,
That a poor fellow-mortal thus should fall!
Let's look at this a moment, Christian friends,
By the clear light that gilds the sacred page.
Are we not here responsible, at least
In some degree, for his dark, tragic end?
Has all been done in word or kindly deed,
As we have met him in our daily walks
And seen him struggling with the adverse tide

Of unkind fortune, battling for his life
Like some lone bark upon a rough lee shore,
Her anxious pilot straining every nerve
To escape the savage rocks and threatening waves,
Now gaining slightly, and then losing more,
Until a blast more unrelenting still
Dispels all hope, and, dashed upon the coast,
The gallant vessel is forever lost?
So he, hard driven on life's stormy sea,
Though long and manfully he did contend,
And not till every cord was torn away
Yielded his post — amid the breakers fell,
And sank within their dark, ingulfing depths.
Not hopeless, though heart-stricken, weeping friends:
Ah! no, God in his mercy, and not man,
Decides our fate, and He who while on earth
Sought the unfortunate and tempest-tost,
Whose sojourn here was marked by love divine
And deeds of mercy at his every step,
Ne'er turned a deaf ear to the sorrowing soul;
And that within us, prompting oft the tear
Of sympathy, comes from a sacred source,
And speaks as sure as words of holy writ,
That love and mercy rule alone in Heaven.
Peace then to thee! no longer poor and lone;

But by the gentle hand of Him who died
That all might live, raised from thy lowly bed,
And washed from every taint, presented pure
At the All-Father's ever-sheltering shrine.

IN MEMORIAM.

—

A. T. T.

OBIIT XIX DIE APRILIS, MDCCCLXVIII,

ÆT. LI.

—

TENDERLY, lovingly, hopefully, bury him,
  So good and so gentle, so manfully true:
Gone in his prime, and day of best usefulness—
  Faded and gone! from our homes and our view.
Alas! what keen anguish, how bitterly wretched,
  That his life should a burden and a pain only prove!
Yet, doubtless, good angels with open arms welcomed
        him,
  And the great All-Father, to his bosom of love:
For if I, a poor mortal, can feel naught but kindness
  And sympathy, flowing from one common bloo
How much more supremely our own blessed Saviour,
  How much deeper and kinder our own gracious God!
Then with blessings upon his last earthly pillow,
Let us hang, mid our tears, his harp on the willow.

THE OLD BARN.

NO hay upon its wide-spread mows,
　　No horses in the stalls,
No broad-horned oxen, sheep, or cows,
　　Within its time-worn walls:

The wind howls through its shattered doors,
　　Now swinging to and fro;
And o'er its once frequented floors
　　No footsteps come or go.

O once, alas! each vacant bay,
　　And every space around,
Was teeming with sweet-scented hay,
　　The harvest of the ground;

And well-fed cattle in a row,
　　At mangers ranged along,
Each fastened by an oaken bow,
　　Stood at the stanchions strong.

But where so long old Dobbin stood,
　　His master's pride and care,

And from whose hand received his food,
   All now is vacant there.

Then these broad fields, from hill to plain,
   Waved in the Summer air
With choicest crops of grass or grain,
   Now left so bleak and bare ;

The swallows chattered· all day long,
   As they flew out and in,
While from their nests on high, the young
   Kept up a constant din ;

The black-bird hailed the dewy morn,
   From out his rushy perch ;
The sparrow sang upon the thorn,
   The cat-bird on the birch ;

The robin from the highest tree
   Sent forth his whistle clear,
·His soul partaking of the glee
   That wakes the vernal year ;

And childhood's merry shout was heard,
   The farm-yard choir among,

Which, mingled with the note of bird,
  Enriched the tide of song;

The lilies bloomed upon the pond,
  Amid the meadows gay,
And scented all the air around,
  Throughout the Summer day.

A pleasant sight it was to see
  The great hay-loaded wain,
With youthful rustics in their glee,
  Come down the rural lane;

The oxen's backs half covered o'er
  With locks of fragrant clover,
The farmer's precious Winter store,
  When sterner toils are over.

And when the Autumn days had come,
  And loudly piped the jay, —
The cheery days of harvest-home, —
  The crops all stored away, —

A happy scene then, the old barn, —
  A joy to young and old,

To strip the yellow shining corn,
  The farmer's ready gold;

The merry jokes around would crack,
  And merry peals of laughter
The old walls gratefully sent back,
  And every beam and rafter.

How sweet the music of the flail,
  Resounding far and clear,
As borne upon the passing gale
  It reached the distant ear!

The master on his daily round
  With conscious pride would go,
His faithful dog close by him found,
  Attending to and fro.

Old honest Trip long since has gone,
  And moulders 'neath the wall;
No more he takes the welcome bone,
  Or hears his master's call.

The kindly master too has died,
  The matron in her grace;

And dead, or scattered far and wide,
  The remnant of their race.

But peace and blessings on the past,
  The poet now would say;
Our joy cannot forever last,
  Nor sorrow ever stay.

1867.

THE MOTHER'S VOICE.

HER voice is like the Dorian flute,
  Heard stealing o'er Arcadian plains,
When e'en the zephyr's sound is mute,
  And twilight in sweet silence reigns.

So soft, so low, it moves the ear,
  And lulls the mind in sweet repose;
It banishes all pain or fear,
  And peace within the bosom flows.

The strongest power in Heaven is Love;
  On earth it still remains the same;
And harmless are the shafts of Jove,
  Before Jehovah's living flame.

So in the heart of each and all,
  Where love and gentleness prevail,
The ruder world is held in thrall,
  And no base passions can assail.

1868.

IN REMEMBRANCE.

J. T.

DIED APRIL 27, 1861, AGED 63 YEARS.

HERE is where we used to rest,
　Uncle James and I;
Our seat the stone with mossy crest,
　Our roof the arching sky.

Around us spread the spacious woods,
　Afar from town and noise,
Within whose grateful solitudes
　We found our quiet joys.

Year after year, in rich content,
　We traced their lonely aisles,
Nor heedless of the blessings sent
　Through Nature's genial smiles.

1868.

TO THE SAME.

THE wood-paths now are growing up,
　　Which we so often threaded;
Our favorite seats, on stump or stone,
　　With leaves and moss are bedded.

Alone I wander through the woods,
　　Where once we roamed so cheerly,
But miss within their solitudes
　　The charms we loved so dearly.

No more the wild flower brings, as wont,
　　Its store of wealth and glory;
Its beauty only lures me now,
　　As some remembered story.

I fancy he is by my side,
　　And strive to keep him near me;
I think I hear his gentle voice,
　　That had such power to cheer me.

But soon I find it all in vain, —
　　That I am only dreaming,

L

And that which was a present good
Is only now a seeming.

But dear in memory shall he
Remain with me forever ;
And though our bodies parted be.
Our spirits naught can sever

1869..

THE WINTER EVENING.

O PLAY again that grand old tune,
　　Resounding far through memory's halls,
Refreshing as the breeze of June
　　Mid songs of birds and waterfalls.

It takes me back to other days,
　　When, void of every earthly care,
I sped amid the giddy maze,
　　In time to that old favorite air.

How jocund passed the light-winged hours,
　　Where youth and beauty led the dance!
Our pathway then was strewn with flowers —
　　The happy season of romance.

O fairy form! O gentle heart!
　　Where have your light and beauty gone?
Do others now like grace impart?
　　Or with the past have all these flown?

Ah, no! kind nature keeps her own,
　　And youth and beauty take the place

Of those from whom these gifts have gone,
    And are renewed in every race;

And glowing eyes and waving hair,
    The kindly voice and lovely smile,
Do still the same attractions wear,
    And still the heart from pain beguile.

Rejoice! then, ye of hopeful years, —
    O! sing and dance while yet you may;
Nor let your hearts, disturbed by fears,
    Look forward to a sadder day.

Strike up the old familiar air,
    And let our hearts to-night rejoice;
A farewell let us give to care,
    And in the song blend every voice.

Tune up, dear hearts, each tuneful throat!
    It is your mother's natal day;
Her voice still with your own shall float,
    As sweet as ere her hair was gray.

And though our years are gathering fast,
    We will to-night be young again,

Again live o'er the sacred past,
    And bid good-by to care and pain.

Blow! winter wind — we dread you not —
    And spread your snow upon the ground,
While safe within our rural cot,
    Among our treasures, we are found.

Our cattle all are housed and fed;
    The barn-yard fowl have gone to rest;
Old "Billy" has his clean straw bed,
    And blanket strapped across his breast.

The sheds well filled with oak and pine,
    Cut from the woods a year ago;
Our household comforts all combine
    To keep aloof the frost and snow.

Thanks to a kindly Father's hand,
    Thanks unto Him who rules above,
Our lot is cast in this fair land,
    Mid scenes that we so dearly love.

While we forget not in our prayer
    Those who to-night are on the sea,

And from our store afford a share
  To meet the claims of poverty, —

Remember still those who so late
  In bonds groaned on our Southern soil,
And by the treachery of state
  Are now oppressed by want and toil.

Blow, Boreas, from your ice-bound sphere,
  And ring your chords among our trees ;
Sound forth the wailings of the year,
  Where sang so late the Summer breeze.

Come, Ranger ! leave the glowing hearth,
  Where you so long have dreamed and slept ;
The cat and kittens join in mirth ;
  'T is time your watch and ward were kept.

Old Ranger 'neath the dresser sneaks,
  With wagging tail and upturned eye —
In vain his master sharply speaks,
  For all exclaim, "O ! let him lie ! "

Yes, lie thou shalt, now stiff and old ;
  Naught shall subject thee to the storm :

Thou once wast like a lion bold,
  Of stately port and graceful form.

So let the storm blow wildly out,
  And howl and whistle at our ears;
Our social bliss will put to rout
  And drive afar all idle fears.

Then heap the wood upon the fire!
  And send a glow on all around!
Let all within to mirth conspire!
  Let merriment to-night abound!

Ye tranquil hours, supremely blessed,
  Dear to my heart — a present heaven —
When no rude passions stir the breast,
  And all is calm as Summer even!

What, then, are riches? what is fame?
  The one takes wings and flies away;
The other glitters in a name,
  And only lives its poor, brief day.

How sweet the boon of rural peace,
  That soothes and heals the wounded heart!

May thy sweet influence never cease ;
  May thou and I ne'er have to part.

Dear quiet haunts, where nature smiles,
  And o'er her votary kindly flings
Her genial blessings, and beguiles
  The heart that listens as she sings, —

Her song of truth and beauty tell,
  And speak the great, good Giver's praise !
From mountain top to shady dell
  All things the glorious anthem raise.

O mellowed days ! O hallowed shrines !
  Where hearts in peace together dwell ;
Around which memory entwines,·
  And bids the soul with pleasure swell !

Ah ! what were life without the power
  To call to mind our happier days,
While waiting for that holier hour
  When we shall join the song of praise ?

Then pleasant pictures let us strive
  Upon life's canvas oft to paint,

Where we again the past may live,
  Though age may make them worn and faint.

With hope triumphant in the heart,
  A trust that all is ordered right,
They who to others joy impart,
  Shall find their waning years more bright.

In chorus shout the brave old air
  That hath awaked this happy vein!
Give vent to joy, farewell to care,
  And yield to love's supernal reign.

1868.

•A RURAL SKETCH.

ON yonder hill an ancient farm-house stands,
With its old barn and sheds, and crib for corn ;
A broad o'ershadowing elm droops near the roof,
And sweeps the mossy shingles with its boughs.
Green meadows and old fields stretch far away,
Bounded by towering woods of oak and pine, —
A pleasant picture 'neath the Summer sky,
Seen from the lowlands on its southern marge.
And with the song of bird and insect hum,
I hear the thumping of the busy flail,
A pleasant music in this rustic scene ;
And just descry between the opening trees,
Within the old barn's broad-spread open doors,
The lusty threshers eager at their toil.
A group of rustic children in the shade,
All brown with berrying in the neigbboring field,
Are making merry on the short green grass.
Beneath a maple's shade in yonder mead,
A group of cattle seek the cooling breeze,
Some standing and some lying down at ease ;
The old horse just apart, resting one foot,

Stands listless ; — nearer, a few straggling sheep,
The wether's tinkling bell just faintly heard,
Browse the short grass upon a verdant knoll ;
While all around the air is calm and sweet,
And overhead the clear blue sky outspread,
With fleecy clouds carcering to the breeze —
The upper current felt not here below.
But hark ! how sweetly comes that pastoral song,
Greeting my ear from yonder rustic path,
Where I behold, returning to her home
From the near village, fairer than all else,
Her father's pride, the graceful Margaret,
Whose golden locks gleam with the flecks of light
That find their way among the shady boughs,
And her fair neck like ivory shines beneath !
How light her step as now she mounts the stile
Upon the turfy bank close at the garden-gate !
Too soon to vanish from my raptured gaze.
In vain shall fashion, with her gaudy show,
Attempt to vie with Nature, ever true
To the great laws that govern man and beast.
From homes like this come forth New England's sons
And daughters, each noble in their own sphere,
And giving dignity and grace where'er
They mingle, whether in the town,

The busy city, or in rural scenes ;
Hence come our sweetest poets, for the muse
Delights to favor those of simple lives,
Who grow up 'neath broad skies in Nature's school,
And drink at wellsprings of eternal truth.
Thus have I painted, in my homely way,
A scene such as may oft be witnessed
By those whose eyes are open to its charms, —
A blessing on them, wheresoe'er they be.

1868.

THE OLD HOMESTEAD.

A PLAIN old-fashioned country house
Was that where I was born,
Built by my grandsire in his prime —
A hundred years agone.

As story goes, the trees were felled
Upon the very spot,
From which its sturdy frame was hewed,
E'en now unharmed by rot —

But fresh and strong as on the day
The huge oak beams were raised,
And hence another hundred years,
By poet may be praised.

The massive chimney, built of brick,
With heavy stone foundation,
Suggested heaping piles of wood,
And heaping stock of ration:

The deep, broad kitchen fire-place,
With oven in its back,

And o'er its high-raised mantel-piece,
  The queer old roasting-jack:

While in the garret far above,
  A wheel and rope were found,
By which the meat upon the spit
  Was slowly turned around.

The floor of pine, so nice and clean,
  And freshly sanded o'er,
The great high settle ranged along
  Between the fire and door,

Bespoke of comfort and good cheer,
  In those rare days of old,
While far around, the blazing hearth
  Kept off the winter's cold.

How cracked the wood upon the fire,
  In ample armfulls thrown!
And roaring up the chimney flue,
  Made music of its own.

A broadened circle thus was made,
  As all sat round the fire, —

The serving-maid and serving-man,
 Grandame, and child, and sire.

The grandsire smoked his long-stemmed pipe
 Within his corner snug,
While on the hearth the apples hummed,
 And eke the cider mug.

The grandame on the other side,
 With knitting-work in hand ;
The tallow candles, nicely dipped,
 Upon the ancient stand —

Where oft the open Bible lay,
 Or book of early Friend,
Whose honest pages lure me still,
 And sweet instruction lend :

For of that simple, Christ-like faith,
 Our ancient household were ;
And " thee," and " thou," and " thus he saith,"
 Evinced our Quaker sphere.

And standing near, the rustic child,
 With open eyes and ears,

Enjoyed the comfort of the scene,
  Nor dreamed of boding fears.

The mottled cat, so fat and sleek,
  Sat purring near the stand;
The old dog stretched himself and yawned,
  And licked the proffered hand.

And so the evening passed away,
  The apples passed around,
The cider in the earthen mug,
  And thus the day was crowned.

O peaceful days, my childhood's boon!
  In memory ever dear;
And dear the plain and honest ways
  That keep our lives from fear.

'T was pleasant, of a " First-day " morn,
  To see the good old pair,
Together in the square-topped chaise,
  With Dobbin plump and fair,

Set off for meeting far away,
  Some six or seven miles:

For where the conscience guides the heart,
　No trifling space beguiles.

A worthier or happier sect
　Than were our ancient sires,
Are found not in the lists of fame
　A grateful world admires.

And fondly still in memory's page
　I keep my childhood's home,
Though many changes, sad and sore,
　Upon its walls have come.

But, in the ever mellowed past
　All things are as before,
And forms and faces meet my gaze
　As they were seen of yore.

Far back into the storied past
　I peer with curious eyes,
To earlier days than those I knew,
　And live 'neath earlier skies.

I still can see the broad domain,
　The spacious fields and woods ;

And mid our crowded city streets
  Form sylvan solitudes ;

Can see the old house, stark and lone,
  Its overshading trees ;
Can hear the robin's evening song,
  And feel the summer breeze ;

Can hear the mowers whet their scythes,
  The dewy herds-grass fall,
And from the old rail-fence beyond,
  The quail his covey call.

My grandsire with his broad-brimmed hat,
  In shirt-sleeves with his men,
Stands leaning on his rake or fork,
  Beside the loaded wain.

Methinks 't was fairer then than now,
  That life was freer then,
And more of faith and honest cheer
  Among the sons of men.

Our lineage boasts no wealth nor rank —
  A simple, honest race,

Who from old England's sea-girt shores
   Their Saxon offspring trace;

Who some two hundred years ago
   Sought out this peaceful nook,
And o'er the broad Atlantic wave,
   Their native land forsook.

And here they made a pleasant home,
   And here, their roofs were reared,
And here, the offshoot of their toil,
   Our city has appeared.

The axe rang through the grand old woods,
   And laid its monarchs low:
No qualms of conscience then held back
   The settler's sturdy blow:

For where was all one savage waste,
   And wild men still around,
The clearings then were pleasant spots,
   And dear the naked ground.

The fields of grain soon rose to view;
   And soon the orchards fair,

And signs of industry and thrift,
  Were scattered here and there.

Along the river's pleasant banks,
  How fair the landscape glowed,
When lighted by the morning sun,
  Its varied beauties showed!

Here by the shore were built the ships
  Which brought our early wealth;
While from the dotted farms around
  Were found the stores of health.

But simple truth is still the same,
  And they who love its ways
Will find its blessings still abound,
  As in those early days.

1868.

A PORTRAIT.

SOBERED by time, a plain and thoughtful man,
  In russet garb of quaint and homely style,
Within the angle of a moss-clad wall,
O'erhung by trees, sits down to rest alone
And meditate, leaning upon his staff,
A rustic stick cut from the neighboring wood.
A glow of health still marks his furrowed face,
For he hath striven through his gathered years
To keep the laws of temperance and peace,
And sought to learn philosophy divine.
Around him spread the fields, and o'er the wall,
For miles away, the old woods stretch along.
Here through the ancient paths he loves to stroll,
When blow the Autumn winds, or Winter rude
With storms of snow drives o'er the rigid plains ;
But most when gentle Spring again returns,
And song of birds awakes the newborn year.
Endeared to him the robin's early note,
The thrush, the jay, and e'en the noisy crow,
The blue-bird's warble, and the sparrow's hymn.
Though not unsocial, yet his soul requires

Long periods of rest from much society,
And mid his books alone he oft is found,
Retired within his humble, snug retreat,
Where naught but homely comforts meet the eye,
And where the poor and weary wayfarer
May find a seat, or those of modest views
A welcome.   Here he sits and writes or reads,
And sometimes falls into a revery
Or slumber.   The rostrum or busy mart
No charm presents to him.   Others may seek
The plaudits of the crowd, but quietude
And meditation mark his peaceful way.
So would he pass through life, and at its close
Trust to that mercy which forgiveth all,
And thus within kind Nature's fostering arms,
His work all finished, close his eyes in peace.

1868.

THE OLD FRIENDS' MEETING-HOUSE.

UPON a gently sloping, grassy knoll,
    Far from the busy town, its dust and noise,
Amid its ancient trees of oak and pine,
Alone the gray old building stands, — comely
And large, for in those happier days,
Ere yet sectarianism had prevailed,
No other meeting through the country wide
For miles around was held, excepting this,
Where the calm followers of Fox and Penn
Assembled, and in silence, or in words
Of simple truth, unmarked by classic lore,
Taught the rude people ways of peace and love.
Nearly two hundred years ago the spot
Was chosen, and here the house was builded,
The first for worship of Almighty God
Within our ancient township, then a part
Of " the Old Colony," and Dartmouth named.
Here mid the wild woods, and still wilder men,
Came our forefathers from old England's shores,
A stalwart race, undaunted by their toil
Or hardship on the ocean or the land.

Here old Ralph Russell, him of Monmouthshire,
Set up his " iron-forge," at that sweet spot
Since known as " Russell's Mills " — a favorite haunt
For lovers of the picturesque and bold
In Nature's works, here so supremely rich,
Where ponderous rocks and beetling cliffs abound.
And here beside the Pascamanset dwelt
The ancestors of those who bear the names
Since so well known within the neighboring town —
The busy mart of ships and merchandise, —
Names spread in numerous progeny about.
These sought a quiet home, where they could live
Without disturbance from the church or state.
A peaceful and industrious race were they,
Who in their simple faith deemed every day,
And all times, as the Lord's, and no one day
Set forth as better, holier than the rest.
And so upon the " First day " of the week,
When all their meeting rites had been performed,
They spent a few hours at its peaceful close
In agricultural labor — hoeing corn,
Or weeding in the garden, doing chores, —
Or visiting a neighbor far away.
These acts the stern old Puritans pleased not,
And so an order from their court was sent,

No further to profane the Sabbath-day ;
And furthermore, to pay the appointed tax
Levied for the support of their own church.
This the Friends refused, and firmly withheld,
Till time and better laws made them exempt.
Constant unto their faith, duly they came
On the First day and Fourth day of the week ;
E'en in the busy harvest-time they came,
For wherein conscience bade them to obey,
None were more faithful.   Here they loved to meet,
And in the stillness of this rural spot,
Where songs of birds, and the soft passing breeze,
From the blue waters of the neighboring bay,
Swept through the boughs, brought music to their ears,
Methinks far sweeter than the loud-voiced choir
Or deep-toned organ.   Here they learned to live
In peace, and often felt, I ween,
The thanks of gratitude rise in the soul.
Here in those early days, from o'er the sea,
Those faithful servants of the Lord, heralds
Of peace and love, the travelling preachers
Of this their newly risen sect, would come : —
Good Thomas Story, the gentle and learned,
And Samuel Bownas, valiant and strong of soul,
Liberal in faith and sound in judgment,

M

Setting aright the simple people here
In a small matter which their body vexed, —
For even then, as now, trifles of discipline
Would breed a discord with the exacting few ;
But in the main a most exemplary sect
The Friends, and to my heart's best pulses dear
The simple faith my fathers learned of old.
Here too that meek disciple of the Lord,
That holy man, an image of the truth,
Beloved Woolman, came, and left his impress
On the more humane : for at that dark day,
Ere yet the nation, or the church itself,
Had given freedom to the poor bondman,
Through the blest influence of this godly man,
And his compeer, the noble Benezet,
Thus early did the Friends release their slaves,
And gave them succor with their liberty.
Then too in later days came those of calmer mould,
Among whom Scott, a man of faith and power,
Who found an honored grave on Erin's shores,
Whence he had gone in service of his Lord.
And he, the sweetest spirit of them all,
Thornton, my grandsire's venerated name,
The Heaven-endowed preacher and poet,
Teacher too of young and old, eloquent

Chanter of inspired truth, tender of heart,
And full of all humanity and love;
No bigotry e'er found in him a place,
But Christ-like charity and living faith.
Time-honored house, so pleasant, so retired —
Though many miles away from my own home,
I love to jog along the country roads
With honest Dobbin of a First-day morn,
By pleasant farms, whose broad-spread fields bespeak
Of wholesome fare, and simple, virtuous lives,
And take a seat within the ancient walls,
Where sat my ancestors in by-gone days.
Here I can listen to " the still, small voice,"
That speaks unto the soul attuned to hear;
And, while the birds are singing in the trees,
And the wind sways the branches to and fro,
The gentle river murmuring on its course,
Disturbing not, but adding to the calm
And solemn stillness of the dear old place,
Find strength and consolation for my soul,
Thus reassuring my too wavering faith.
Here let me still resort, and with the few
Who yet remain, the remnant of the band
So strong and numerous once, join in worship,
Or at least refresh my lagging spirit.

And here at times, while musing on the past,
I people, as of old, the vacant seats,
And fancy I can see the company
That once assembled, filling every space, —
While in the " gallery " some preacher strong,
From far-off Britain or a distant State,
Is holding forth in gospel power the truth,
Such as at Athens Paul himself proclaimed —
The eager listeners drinking every word,
Fresh from the fountain of renewing life.
O ! blame me not, ye of sterner cast,
Who keep a check on every roving thought,
That I thus idly should employ the time
Intended for a higher, holier cause ;
For to my soul, religion, stripped and robbed
Of poetry and grace, is half destroyed.
God gave us life — He gave us, too, these gifts,
Not to be despised, but ever used aright ;
And he who crushes in his inmost soul
The gentler promptings, does a violence
To truth and beauty, and a bankrupt proves
Of earth's best riches.   O, may never here
The pride of bigotry and ignorance
Approach !   The very trees themselves, the air,
The birds, and, too, the murmuring river,

The chirp of insect, and the floating clouds
That sail across the vast cerulean deep,
All speak of liberty and present love.
Sacred, then, to peace and sweet religion,
Such as the Saviour, were he here on earth,
Would recognize, let this old house remain.

1868.

THE SHANTY.

IN this little calm retreat
  How much peace and joy I find;
Solitude may thus be sweet,
  If it does not cramp the mind,

But give knowledge to impart
  Unto others favored less,
Truths that sanctify the heart,
  Wisdom that our God will bless.

1868.

OUR VILLAGE.

NESTLED among its fields and neighboring woods,
    Along the river's pleasant banks it stands,
A simple rural hamlet; yet, forsooth,
In bygone days a scene of busy life,
Through which the stage-coach, passing to and fro,
Stopped at the tavern, took and left the mail,
And travellers upon their dusty way
In Summer, or in Winter's stormy time,
Found a retreat both for themselves and beasts;
But now a kind of " Sleepy Hollow," where
The tired stranger finds no hostelry,
Yet food and lodging 'neath some humble roof,
Such as the homely comfort of the place affords,
And better, doubtless, than where greater show
With vain pretence so oft deludes the guest,
Exacting much, with little in return.
But further to describe, let me proceed : —
Two houses placed at either end stand forth,
Where faithfully the gospel is proclaimed :
The followers of Wesley and Calvin
Here abide in peace.   And farther on,

Upon the hill, a plain and time-worn house
Is seen, where meet as wont a little band
Of those called Quakers, once numerous here,
Before schisms unfortunate sundered them
And scattered far and wide their sturdy ranks.
Near by an ancient grave-yard, with its stones
Dating far back to the first settlement
Of this ancestral town, then Dartmouth called,
Rests on the hill-top, mid o'ershading trees.
Here too once stood a comely edifice,
Where a famed preacher taught his numerous flock,
The grandsires of a far-spread progeny.
But Nature still her faith and beauty holds,
And standing on the river's upland banks,
A varied scene presents itself to view, —
Green fields and orchards, woods and groves around,
The village lying in the vale below,
The graceful church-spire shooting far above
The humbler houses, and before them all
A striking feature of this rural scene,
The river gliding onward to the sea,
Homes of rural comfort seen here and there,
And far away the city with its spires,
Its dust and clamor lost upon the air.
Just at the bridge, and near the river bank,

Stands a rude building, ancient, dark, and low,
Yet of no small importance in its time;
And though so rude and rough, and worn with age,
A cheerfulness is often found within,
When the huge bellows kindle up its fires,
And the old forge, refulgent in the blaze,
Sends all around a warm and pleasant light,
That makes old Winter, in his stormy reign,
Yield half his terrors to the genial heat
Which thus from honest industry obtains.
See how beneath the ponderous iron sledge,
Wielded by arms of herculean strength,
The meteoric shower flies through the air;
Anon replacing with his needful tongs
The cooling iron, now the brawny arm
Leans on the brake, attentive to his task,
While rushing down the creaking bellows pipe
Comes the enkindling draft, making all glow.
There with his swarthy brow, dishevelled hair,
Broad chest, and broad, expressive face,
Stands one who from his youth to manhood's prime
Hath by this ancient craft his living gained, —
A son of Vulcan, but of kindly mien.
Skillful at shoeing oxen, oft I've seen
The patient victim slung, and strong-armed John

Setting the shoe and driving in the nail,
The sweat careering down his honest face,
While patiently some honest Dobbin stands
Waiting his turn, his master at the door,
Or seated at the forge smoking his pipe,
And chatting of the times with an old friend,
Or with the Squire, who on his daily round
Has stopped to chat on politics or news —
No theme too trite to occupy the hour,
And loud the laughter at the ancient joke,
Told for the hundredth time to listening ears.
So passes on the peaceful village life,
And when good feelings and good will prevail,
More to be envied than the stormy mart,
Where men with sharpened wits together come,
And by their wits their fortunes make or lose.
For me the quiet of the fields and woods,
And rural occupations lure my hours,
Where studious of good I hope to learn,
And learning to secure immortal bliss.
In former days, ere yet our river's course
Had been obstructed by the miller's dam,
The shad, the herring, and the salmon too,
Were in abundance, and e'en now at times,
When Spring once more gives life afresh to all

M2

Animate and inanimate creation,
Following their instinct schools of herring,
And occasionally a shad, appear.
Then all the village youths with ample nets
Stand at the bridge or by the river's marge,
Mostly at evening, eager for their prey:
A cheerful sight, and often I have stopped
Upon my evening walk to see their sport,
Wondering if those born of hardier nerves
Feel not, when struggling for their liberty
The glittering victims in their baskets lie.
Here once in years long passed away
The Britons, landing on our southern shore,
Marched some four thousand, halting at this spot,
And pillaging and burning on their way,
Drove the unarmed villagers to the woods
And other places of retreat.   Those days
Are passed, and all of that old race
Who tilled the soil or labored at their trades
Have also passed away.   Thus time goes on,
And generation after generation
Move o'er the scene of action and are gone.
O, mid these peaceful realms where Nature kind
Hath outspread so much wealth and beauty
In varied landscape, hill and dale, and stream,

And made a healthful home for man and beast,
May never war or waste or bitterness
With blighting steps pass o'er, but kindly still
The song of labor, roused in happy hearts,
Rise at morning's and the evening's close.

MEMORIES.

HOW sweetly over the noise and the clamor
   Sounds the clear note of the robin above,
Above in the limbs of the old rotten plane-tree,
   Notes fitting the lute of an angel of love.

And fondly remembered, the days of my boyhood
   Come back with the songs of the sweet vernal choir,
A freshness and richness no treasure surpasses,
   And that they may last is my soul's deep desire.

THE DESERTED FARM-HOUSE.

A HUNDRED years and more the smoke
    Had gone forth day by day
From out that ancient chimney's throat,
    Upon its devious way.

And all throughout that lengthened time
    The years have come and gone
In sweet accord with Nature's chime,
    A music of her own.

But now no fire upon the hearth
    Sends round its cheerful glow;
No sound of childhood's noisy mirth
    As erst is heard to flow.

The path across the neighboring field,
    Once used and well defined,
Is daily growing more obscure,
    And erelong none we'll find.

The snows drift at the time-worn steps,
    And block the fastened door,
Or through the rattling windows drives
    Upon the vacant floor.

The sweep and pole now listless hang
  Above the mossy well,
While to its once frequented fount
  The path no footsteps tell.

The garden too, the household pride,
  Where earliest simples grew,
Now lies neglected and forlorn,
  No longer fair to view.

Against the chimney's weather side
  The snow and ice remain,
No warmth within its spacious walls
  To melt them off again.

The moon looks through the frosty panes,
  And lights the silent room,
But only makes more clearly seen
  The solitude and gloom.

Where once the aged couple sat
  Beside the glowing fire,
All now is chill and desolate,
  And gone the worthy sire.

How cheerful here in days gone by,
  To memory ever dear,

The household hum of industry,
  When naught was felt of fear!

The matron at her daily task
  Their frugal comfort sought,
While at his labor in the field
  Or wood the good-man wrought.

Throughout the pleasant Summer days
  The bee sung 'mong the flowers,
As passed beneath this happy roof
  The swift, light-footed hours.

And when the stormy Winter winds
  Swept o'er the whitened earth,
How cracked and glowed the burning logs
  Upon the ample hearth!

But like all other things of life,
  These scenes have passed away,
Yet in his goodness God remains
  To bless us day by day.

  1868.

THE MINISTRY OF NATURE.

ALONE with Nature and with God,
  I sit down more secure
Than in the temple's cushioned seat,
  With countenance demure.

I need no aid of human voice,
  Nor organ loudly sounding,
While God is chanting in the breeze,
  His present grace abounding.

I scorn not vocal prayer and praise,
  The heart's poor honest striving,
While many souls are in this way
  Their daily food deriving;

But when I hear through oak and pine
  Their sympathies so wakeful,
I find a solace in my heart
  That bids me to be grateful.

Though Winter still is lingering here,
  The day is soft and vernal,

And everything around bespeaks
  Of Him, the Good Eternal.

The little chickadee, that hops
  From branch to branch so cheerly,
Gives me a lesson of content
  That I would value dearly.

The lichens on the old oak trees,
  That smile so fresh and greenly,
Teach wisdom in the humblest things,
  And move the heart serenely.

Then often hither let me hie,
  When sad or worn and weary,
And seek within these sacred haunts
  The good so fair and cheery.

1869.

WHITTIER AND LONGFELLOW.

BRAVE singers in our western world are ye,
 Each in his own inspired strains exceeding;
Who both have sung of Nature, broad and free,
 And both have helped to heal our nation's bleeding.

How glorious, in the early days of youth,
 Those halcyon days with music ever ringing,
Came to your listening souls the golden truth,
 With sacred interest through the ages singing.

The one in Nature's school almost alone
 Found the rare lore with beauty ever teeming,
The other partly at fair learning's throne,
 But most from Nature in his young soul beaming.

No warrior wreath may sit upon your brows, —
 But conquerors still in your own peaceful way,
By that sweet spirit which the soul endows,
 And rules the world with more than regal sway.

1869.

A HUNDRED YEARS AGO.

A HUNDRED years ago! where are they now
　　Who then walked on the earth? Not one is found
　　found
Within this wide domain wherein I dwell.
Of all the thousands that began their life,
How few in the whole world can now be found!
But Nature is unchanged, — she keeps her own,
And only where man interferes, remains
As fresh and beautiful as at the first.
That shining stream, that mossy rock,
The song of bird, the wild flower in its bloom,
The overarching sky, the moon and stars,
And the great orb of day, remain the same.
E'en yon old farm-house has outlived by far
Its ancient tenant, and that aged man
Whom now I see passing within its door,
Is grandson of the first who called it home.
So passes man, — so shall we all pass off
The stage of action ; happy then if we
Enact our part acceptably to Him
Who ruleth all things, and sustains in love

This habitable globe and myriad worlds.
Dear Nature, and dear Framer of it all,
My soul would render thanks for blessings rare,
And hope for mercy and a peaceful close,
Mid scenes of rural beauty where so long
A pilgrim pensioner I have sojourned.

1868.

TO WILLIAM BARNES,

AUTHOR OF "RURAL POEMS."

PERMIT a stranger o'er the Atlantic wave,
　　Like thee a lover of calm rural life
And Nature in her simplest charms arrayed,
One who loves quiet hours and quiet hearts,
The simple melodies of wood and field,
And wild flowers blooming in their snug retreats,
To welcome thee as with a brother's hand,
And thank thee with the fervor of a heart.
Ever alive to kindly sympathies,
For thy sweet rural lays, songs of such cheer,
That to my mind a richer influence lend
Than stately epics wreathed in mystic lore ;
For I am but a man, a common man,
And with the old Roman poet-slave,
" Nothing that 's human foreign is to me " ;
And thus the every-day affairs of life,
The homely joys and sorrows of mankind,
The haunts of man, his home, his resting-place,
Are objects of my sympathy and love.

The common feelings of the human heart,
The smple ways so sweet of rustic life,
Its daily struggles, mixed with light and shade,
The care for God's inferior animals,
To whom we owe so much, the rural walk
Mid scenes of pastoral life and beauty,
Cottages enshrined in vines, bright flowers
Beside the doorway, and within the home
Cleanliness and thrift, though of a humble sort, —
All these, dear bard, and many more such like,
Thou hast portrayed as with a limner's skill,
And brought thy Dorset pictures to our eyes,
So that we feel a dear congenial soul
Beats in true concord with our grateful hearts.
A welcome then, though in my humble verse,
Would I extend to thee, dear fellow-bard,
And God's best blessings on thy head invoke.

1869.

ASPIRATIONS.

O IN the life that is to come, may I,
    Dear Father, all redeemed by thee from sin,
Not only meet those dear by Nature's ties,
The cherished household band, but also see
Those unto whom my heart so fondly clings,
Whose glorious works have wrought upon my soul
Such happiness from early youth to age.
And first, my much loved Cowper, teacher dear
In wisdom's ways and Nature's fair domains,
Thou gentle spirit unto whom I owe
A debt of gratitude deep and sincere,
For hours of pleasure and instruction wise ; —
How oft with thee upon my rural walks
Have I in sweet communion strolled along
Through fields and woods, or by some murmuring stream !
And felt thy genial sway, O Poesy,
Pervade my mind, enriching all around.
The solemn muse of Young, leading the soul
To look beyond the things of earth to Him
Who ruleth all things by his Sovereign will ;
And tuneful Gray, so mellow and so rich,

Shedding o'er Nature a transcendent calm ;
Thomson, whom early too I learned to love,
And from his Seasons drew a fresh delight ;
Then dear Beattie, with his minstrel harp,
And moral lessons told in graceful verse'; —
And coming down to still more modern days,
Our own rich Wordsworth, simple, and yet deep
In that philosophy which bears aloft
The humblest objects, and enjoins on man
The recognition of her royal truths ; —
And over all great Milton, master of
The lyre, whether its chords resound of life
Or death, or chant of sweet Arcadian scenes,
Perfect in all, and gracefully sublime.
For such companionship my soul aspires
In that blessed land, where peace and virtue reign.
Ask I too much?   O let me then prepare,
By close observance of the heavenly law,
And drinking oft at Siloam's holy fount.
The cleansing waters, and by grace Divine
Washed of all stain, to meet the heavenly host —
The great and good who once dwelt on the earth.
And may I not, dear Father, hope that thou
Wilt hear my prayer for this thy benison,
That while on earth my best companionship

Hath been among the good, so that in heaven
I may renew and add to my erewhile
Friends, such as I have ever found to be,
Whether among the living or the dead,
Congenial to my soul?   And thus shall Heaven
Prove the great fulfilment of my best hopes;
And there, perhaps, my humble rural muse,
By Thy permission graciously vouchsafed,
May join in singing praises unto Thee,
Who out of chaos wrought Thy wondrous works.

1868.